Side-swiped

A novel

Ellen Gardner

i

ISBN 13-978-1719066068
ISBN-10: 171906606X

CreatesSpace, Charleston, SC
Available from Amazon.com and other retail outlets

Dedication

I dedicate this book to my husband, Jerry Hauck,

who has given me my life back.

Acknowledgements

My deepest thanks to all the members of the Talent Writers Group. Your input and encouragement has been invaluable. Special thanks to Patricia Florin for her painstaking line by line editing, to Bob Carter for creating the book cover, and to my husband Jerry for throwing around ideas, some of which made their way into the story.

Side-swiped is a work of fiction. Names, places, and incidents are all products of the author's imagination and any resemblance to actual people, living or dead, is purely coincidental.

Ellen Gardner

You never know how strong you are
until being strong is the only choice you have.

~ Unknown

Ellen Gardner

1

Ernestine Emmons sat at the breakfast table with Walter, her husband of forty-one years. "The kids are talking about giving you a party," she said as she refilled his coffee cup.

"A party for what?"

"Your birthday, silly. You'll be eighty this year, and the kids think we should have a party."

"Bah." Walter laid down the newspaper he'd been reading and scowled. "I don't want any damn party. Tell them to forget it."

"At least think about it, Walter. If you don't want a party, then tell me what you *do* want. Is there something you've always dreamed of doing? Woodworking?

Photography? Fly fishing? Why don't you make a bucket list, like in that Jack Nicholson movie?"

Except for deer hunting in the fall and morning coffee at McDonald's with a bunch of old guys, Walter didn't have anything to do, and Ernestine wasn't exactly thrilled about having him around the house so much of the time. She had her routines, her ways of doing things, and since he retired he was always underfoot, rearranging the dishwasher, or following her around while she cleaned. She couldn't even go to the grocery store without him tagging along. It was damned annoying.

And it wasn't just that. He'd either gotten forgetful or he simply wasn't paying attention. She always had to remind him where he'd left his glasses, his coffee cup, his jacket. And she got tired of answering the same questions over and over again. She told herself he was bored. She thought he needed a hobby.

The hardware store had been his whole life. He'd gone to work there right out of high school and was pretty much running the whole operation by the time the owner retired and offered to sell him the business. He was only thirty-six at the time and buying the store was a huge risk. But it had worked out well. He renamed the store Emmons Home and Garden, and because everybody knew and trusted him, the store became a major player in the community. Walter had put his heart and soul into that store. So much so, that he had little time for anything else. Ernestine expected he would keep on working there until he dropped dead.

When Walmart came in, however, the clientele started to dry up. People wanted to shop at the big store where they could buy groceries, clothes, hunting and fishing supplies, pharmaceuticals, even hardware, all in the same place. Walter had to let some of his employees go, but by then he was in his seventies and he actually enjoyed the slower pace.

That was about the time Leona, the bookkeeper who'd been with him for years, noticed he was making mistakes. Ordering supplies they didn't need, mixing up deliveries, and giving customers bad advice. At Leona's suggestion and with input from others, Ernestine had convinced Walter to retire.

Now, five years later, he was having similar problems with his personal business. Last August he'd gotten a letter from the IRS saying he'd made miscalculations on the tax return he'd filed in April. And just this week, he'd come home from the bank angry because he'd forgotten his pin number and couldn't get any cash.

2

Walter came back from McDonald's one morning, talking about getting an RV, and Ernestine kicked herself for putting the bucket list idea in his head. It seemed his brother-in-law Richard had gotten him all worked up, telling him how much fun he and Shirley were having with theirs.

"Richard and Shirley just got back from the Grand Canyon," Walter said. "That's a place I've always wanted to see."

"When did you decide that?" Ernestine asked. "You've never mentioned it before."

"I've been thinking about it ever since you got me that subscription to *National Geographic*. And hearing Richard and the other guys talk about their trips makes me think we should see all the national parks. Maybe even see the glaciers in Alaska before they're gone."

This desire to travel was news to Ernestine. In all the years they'd been married, he'd never once mentioned the Grand Canyon, or any place else for that matter. She was the one who, years ago, wanted to go places, but with Walter's business tying them down, it never happened. She figured the window of opportunity had closed, much the way she'd once given up expecting she'd have children.

She was thirty-two when she met him. He was almost forty, a well-established businessman anxious to get married and start a family. She'd gotten pregnant right away and her miscarriage was a huge disappointment for both of them, as was the second one a year later. As time went on without another pregnancy, she gradually accepted childlessness as her lot in life, and by the time she was forty, motherhood was the last thing on her mind. When her menstrual periods stopped, she thought she'd started menopause. The news that she was expecting was, well, unexpected.

Her friends made a big deal out of her pregnancy and gave her an elaborate baby shower, but after the excitement of a new baby wore off, she rarely saw any of them. While she was changing diapers and making baby food, her friends were driving their teenagers to football practice and music lessons. Many resumed their careers while she stayed at home with her daughter, and by the time Linda was in her teens, Ernestine felt out of touch and irrelevant. The waitressing work she'd done before marriage had hardly prepared her for a late life career.

Once Walter got the RV bug, he started taking Ernestine around to sales lots, and in spite of herself, she began to get excited too. She hadn't realized how many different kinds of recreational vehicles there were. They looked at camping trailers that you just popped up after you got where you were going, but most of those didn't have a toilet. She insisted on a toilet. Besides, that kind was too small and too basic. There were camper vans, but you had to always be changing things around, making the dinette into a bed and then back into a dinette again when you wanted to eat. She couldn't see spending more than a weekend in one of those.

"If we do this," she told Walter, "we have to get something with a real bed."

"Well, what about one of these?" Walter led her to a class C motorhome that had a ladder going up to a bed over the cab of the truck. Ernestine shook her head. "No way. I'm not climbing a ladder to get to my bed."

For a while Walter's morning coffee group stopped their usual trashing of the government and turned to mentoring Walter on the various types of RVs. Richard's was a Class A motorhome that was as big as a Greyhound bus. He swore it was the only way to go.

Sitting in Walter and Ernestine's living room, their friend Louie expressed a different opinion. He had a fifth-wheel and argued that fifth-wheels made more sense. "Say you're in Arizona and you have engine trouble," Louie said, his cigar moving from one side of his mouth to the other, "well what're you gonna do? If you have one a them Class A one-piece jobs, ya got to get a mo-tel 'cause ya cain't sleep in it settin' there at the re-pair shop. And that's gonna cost ya. But if ya got the fifth-wheel, ya just unhitch it in a campground and while yer truck is gettin' worked on you got a place to stay."

"You make a good point," Walter told him, "but I don't know as I'd be comfortable pulling a big trailer like that. Besides, I'd have to get me a new pickup. I don't think my old Ford has enough power."

"Suit yerself," Louie said. "I'm just sayin'."

When Richard and Walter's sister, Shirley, came for Sunday dinner, they brought a laptop computer and played a slideshow of their trip to the Grand Canyon.

"There we are standing on the rim of the canyon," Shirley said when the first slide came up. "You can't believe how enormous it is. Pictures don't do it justice. You have to see it for yourself."

Each successive slide provoked commentary. Shirley narrated the scenic shots and Richard jumped in whenever the motorhome was in the frame, bragging about the good deal he'd got on it, and how roomy it was inside.

"I'm telling you," Richard said, "you're better off with the kind we have. A fifth-wheel can be a nightmare. Try backing one of them babies up on a narrow road. She'll jack-knife on you and you'll be in one hell of a fix. A motorhome is one piece. Much easier to maneuver."

Ernestine watched and imagined herself and Walter on a trip. The recreational vehicles she'd seen so far were like sweet little dollhouses with upholstery that matched the wall coverings, miniature appliances, and compact bathrooms. She had started to fantasize about the plastic dinnerware she'd buy, what she'd stock in the

7

cupboards, and how she'd make it all homey with plants, and pictures, and books, but the talk of jack-knifing a trailer took the wind out of her sails. Until then she'd never considered the danger involved.

So far every time they'd been approached by a salesman, Walter said, "We're just starting to think about looking," or, "We're not really in the market just yet." But after seeing Richard's slideshow, Walter was ready to get serious.

On Monday they drove to a sales lot where they spent the morning climbing in and out of trailers and motor coaches, one after another, with a grinning salesman—"Call me Bob"—so close he was practically stepping on the heels of Walter's shoes. Every few minutes Bob slapped Walter on the back. "So, Wally, this one's real sweet, ain't she? I could make you a real nice deal."

And every time he did that, Ernestine winced. If there was anything Walter hated, it was being called Wally. She tried to catch the salesman's eye and give him the danger sign, but the guy was ignoring her, tripping along after Walter like a groupie after a rock star.

"Now take a look-see at this one, Wally," Bob said, walking them over to beautiful shiny beige bus with scrollwork painted around the windows and a decal of a leopard on the back.

Ernestine couldn't believe how fancy it was inside. Granite countertops. A luxurious bathroom. A built-in entertainment center with a wide-screen TV. A king-sized bed. Even a computer. Sitting behind the steering wheel, Walter looked like he was born to it, but when

Ernestine sat in the driver's seat, she felt like a little kid in a grown-up's car.

"This is just the ticket don't ya think, Wally? She's like brand new. Old man that bought it had a stroke and his widow was afraid to dri— "

Ernestine had been enjoying herself until the salesman's comment struck at the heart of her fear. "Exactly," she said, tugging on Walter's arm. "Let's go, I don't think this is such a good idea after all."

Bob looked dejected. "Have you thought about a fifth-wheel? You know you get a lot more for your money that way."

"Yeah, I've thought about that," Walter said, "but then I'd have to buy a bigger truck and seems to me it'd come out about the same money-wise. Nope, I think a one-piece is the way to go."

"Well now, we have a Class C that just come in." He pointed to the dusty side lot where the older, smaller vehicles stood. "Maybe that'd be more to the missus' liking."

After they poked their heads in a couple of Class Cs, Walter took Ernestine's arm. "We're done here." They left Bob scratching his head as he watched his commission walk off the lot.

When they were out of Bob's earshot, Ernestine said, "I don't know about this. What if we're off someplace and something happens to you? Who'd drive it? How would we get it home?"

"Nothing's going to happen to me."

"You don't know that. It could. You could hurt your back or you could have a heart attack. That's what happened to Mildred's husband, and they ended up having to stay in that awful New Mexico town where the hospital was just horrible and he almost died. They had that great big motorhome and she was afraid to dri—"

"Whoa, Ernie honey, hold on," Walter took hold of her shoulders. "You're getting yourself all riled up over something that's not going to happen. In the first place nothing is going to happen to me. And in the second place, you aren't Mildred, and you can learn to drive it."

Ernestine took a deep breath and tried to sound calm. "But that one we sat in, I couldn't even reach the pedals. The mirrors were way out to the side where I couldn't have seen what was coming up behind me if I had to."

"Oh, now, you're being silly. Those things can all be adjusted."

3

Walter gave up on RV lots and started searching the newspaper's want ads. That's how they ended up with the thirty-seven-foot Allegro. It wasn't fancy like the ones Ernestine had liked so much, but the price was in line with what Walter said they could afford. And the name, Allegro, appealed to her. It sounded so musical. The inside was done up in pretty pastel colors and it had all the conveniences—a tiny bathroom with a shower, a bed you could get in and out of without crawling over each other, and slide outs for extra space. It was ten years old and clean as new. In fact, Ernestine wondered if it had even been used, if maybe something had happened to the owner and his wife was afraid to drive it.

Once they bought the Allegro, Walter drove it to Richard's place and spent the better part of a day learning how things worked. When he got home, he told Ernestine, "It isn't just a matter of knowing how to drive it. You need to know about the holding tanks for black water and grey water, hookups for the electricity and sewer line, all the chemicals you need to have, the bio-degradable toilet paper—"

"I had no idea it was so complicated," she said. "I'll leave all that to you and I'll get what we need for the inside."

She hadn't gone shopping alone since Walter retired, so she had a great time in the Dollar Store getting sample-sized toiletries, dishtowels, plastic storage containers, and neon-colored dishes. Then she went to Walmart. Pushing her cart through the store, she felt almost giddy as she grabbed things she thought might be useful. She purchased some inexpensive pots, a Teflon skillet, an electric griddle, a four-cup coffee maker, some cutlery, and a several cans of Lysol Disinfectant Spray. And because she feared being caught unawares, she scoured the pharmacy section for every kind of headache, cold, and itch remedy she thought they might need.

On the way home, she pulled into the parking lot of Between the Covers, the used bookstore, and filled a bag with paperback books. Noticing the games section, she got another bag and added a checkers set, a cribbage board, and several packs of playing cards.

"What the hell?" Walter asked, seeing the mountain of shopping bags.

"It's things we're going to need."

"Don't know where you're going to put it all. Not a lot of storage space."

The next morning, after she returned from Trader Joe's, where she'd stocked up on groceries, she started putting things away. Somehow the cabinets and drawers that seemed roomy at first had shrunk to the size of shoeboxes. The bedroom closet was only as wide as her ironing board, and the miniature refrigerator held less than half of what she wanted to put in it. She shoved and jostled and rearranged, and in the end, admitted she'd have to leave a lot of her purchases behind.

The shopping and the exertion of putting it all away, left her looking as frazzled as she felt. She had postponed her beauty parlor appointment, and her usual tidy cap of gray hair was over-long and sticking out in all directions. Walter said she looked like Einstein.

She called Nancy, the woman who had been doing her hair for years. When the salon had raised their prices a while back, Ernestine considered going elsewhere, but the truth was, she loved how Nancy always flattered her and made her feel special.

"He could have knocked me over with a feather," Ernestine gushed the minute Nancy set her in a chair. "A motorhome is the last thing I expected him to want."

"Has he ever mentioned it before?"

"Not once. He never showed any interest in traveling."

"How big is it?"

"Monstrous. Thirty-seven feet, I think."

"That's about the same size as ours," Nancy said. "We love it. You'll have a blast."

"I hope so. It's just that I'm worried about Walter."

"Why? Isn't he well?"

"Oh, he's well all right, just forgetful. But he's eighty years old. If something happens to him, I don't know what I'd do. I had a friend whose husband had a heart attack while they were on a trip. She had to take over the driving and it scared her half to death."

Nancy threw a cape around Ernestine's shoulders. "Oh, honey, don't go borrowing trouble. If you do have to drive it, you'll do fine. It's no different than driving a car. Now, what do want me to do to your hair?"

Ernestine took a deep breath. "Well, I was thinking about having you color it. We're leaving tomorrow and we won't be seeing anybody we know. What do you think? Would it make me look younger?"

"Absolutely. You'd look good as a redhead."

"Really? You think so? I was thinking an ashy blond or—"

"No honey, ash would wash you out. You need something glamorous. Red. Definitely red."

Looking in the mirror afterward, Ernestine was thrilled. "Oh my heavens," she giggled. "I wonder what Walter will say." She gave Nancy an overly generous tip and a hug, and headed home.

When Ernestine came in the back door, Walter called from his recliner, "What's for supper?"

Instead of answering, she walked into the living room and stood in front of his chair, where he was engrossed in a *National Geographic.*

She cleared her throat, and when he didn't look up, she nudged his foot with her knee. When he raised his eyes, the expression on his face was, she thought, one of horror.

"Well?"

Walter let the magazine fall open on his lap. There was a full-color spread with pictures of Sumatran Orangutans, exactly the same color as Ernestine's hair. Walter looked at Ernestine, down at the pictures, and up again.

She followed his eyes. "Okay, go ahead and say it."

"Nope. Not saying a word."

She went to the kitchen and put a casserole in the oven. While it cooked, she made several trips to the bathroom to look in the mirror. Maybe Walter didn't like her hair, but she did.

4

Heading south on I-5 Walter seemed to have everything under control and Ernestine started to relax. She looked at him in his bright green polo, his silver white hair showing around the edges of his new Good Sam Club hat, and thought how handsome he still was at eighty. Unlike her, he was as slim as the day she met him.

Vivian the cat, stretched, sunning herself on the dashboard in front of the steering wheel. Ernestine would have preferred not to bring her along, but planning as they were to be gone for an undetermined amount of time, they didn't have a choice. Vivian was a pretty calico with a black patch over one eye, an orange patch over the other, and a mean streak a mile wide. She'd been a foundling that Walter bottle-fed, and they had bonded. She'd even crawled inside his shirt and tried to nurse a few times. But she and Ernestine were adversaries. Vivian guarded Walter, hissing and even biting Ernestine if she got too close to him.

They'd left home just before noon and Walter estimated their travel time to be two hours, "give or take." All was going smoothly, with Ernestine musing about this, that, and the other. She tilted her seat back and picked up the crossword puzzle from the morning paper.

"The capitol of Mongolia. Nine letters."

"U-L-A-N B-A-T-O-R."

"Wow," she said, scribbling in the letters. "How do you know all that stuff? Here's another one. What's a five-letter word for a highlander with land?"

"L A I R D."

Impressed, she threw out an easy one. "Blank showers bring May flowers?"

"What?"

"Blank showers. Which month is that?"

"I don't know."

"Of course you do."

"I said I don't know." He sounded irritated, so Ernestine put the newspaper aside and flipped down the mirrored sun visor. She'd almost forgotten about the dye job, and her reflection startled her. Suddenly she wished she had waited to change her hair until after their visit with their daughter, Linda, who was sure to have something negative to say about it.

Linda and her husband Matt had recently bought a house in a Sacramento suburb, and Linda was making a birthday dinner for Walter. When Ernestine accepted the invitation, she hadn't mentioned the motorhome. Walter wanted it to be a surprise.

Just south of Woodland, a gust of wind slammed into the side of the Allegro, pushing it into the left-hand lane. The long, straight bridge went on for nearly a mile, with Walter gritting his teeth and gripping the steering wheel, riding the motorhome like a cowboy on a bucking horse. Vivian flattened herself against the windshield just out of Walter's line of sight and Ernestine grabbed the strap above her window and held her breath until they got to the other side of the bridge.

"Oh my God, Walter," she wheezed, "was that supposed to happen?"

Walter shook his shoulders and loosened his grip. "That must be the Elkhorn Bridge," he said. "I read something about high winds on that stretch, but I didn't think much of it."

Taking a deep breath, Ernestine wondered what else Walter had read and not thought much of. The closer they got to Sacramento, the more the traffic picked up. Ernestine gasped every time another car entered the freeway from the right and cut across in front of them, but she didn't say anything for fear of distracting Walter. He stayed in the far right lane and slowed to a crawl. Then realizing at the last minute that it was an exit only lane, he jerked the wheel to the left, narrowly missing the snappy red sports car coming up behind him. The driver laid on his horn and made a rude hand gesture as he passed.

"Okay now," Walter said, "you have the directions. You need to help me watch the signs."

With shaking hands, Ernestine dug around in her pocketbook and pulled out a notepad. "Look for I-80." She leaned forward and watched the signs, yelling "There it is! There it is!" when it came into view. Once they were off on the exit, she felt confident about where they were going. Linda's directions were clear and she'd even sent pictures so they would be able to recognize the house. "We're looking for Madison Avenue. It's a ways, so just keep going until you get to San Juan."

"Okay, then what?"

"I'll tell you when to turn." Ernestine took a breath and consulted her directions again to make sure. She saw the sign for San Juan. "Turn right, now, and then turn left. After that, you need to stay to the right or you'll end up on—"

"Okay, okay," Walter said. "Just tell me when to turn."

"That's it!" Ernestine squealed when they turned and saw the house sitting high off the street above a steep driveway.

Halfway up the driveway, the motorhome bottomed out, making a horrific scraping noise. Walter set the emergency brake and cut the engine.

Linda ran out the front door. "What on earth? Dad, is this yours?" Then before Walter could say anything, she said, "You can't park it there, your rear end is sticking out in the street and you're blocking the driveway. Matt has to get his car out of the garage. He has to go to work."

"Whoa, hold on," Walter said. "Aren't you even going to say hello before you bawl me out?"

"Hello, Dad. But you have to move it."

"Okay, okay, I'll move it as soon as I get my hug." He stood up from the driver's seat and climbed out.

"Seriously, Dad," Linda said, "a motorhome? Don't you think you're too—"

"Wait just a goll darn minute," Walter said, "Don't go telling me I'm too old."

"Sorry." Linda gave him a hug and waited while Ernestine got out. "Oh my God, Mom, what's with the hair?"

Ernestine ignored the remark. "Hello, dear."

"You guys didn't buy this thing, did you?"

"Yes, we did, and we're going to take a road trip."

"Good God. What were you thinking? Where did the money come from? I hope you didn't mortgage the house."

"You know, Linda, that's not your business. Your dad worked his whole life—"

"Yes, and if you let him burn through his retirement, what will you do then?"

"Give him some credit. He knows how to handle money."

"Well it just seems to me... Oh, never mind. But Dad's too old to be driving something this big. I can't believe you let him."

Just then Linda's teenage sons bounced out of the house and started circling the motorhome.

"Hey, Gramps," Jeremy hollered, "great geezer mobile."

"Yeah, totally," Jack shouted, "We see old people driving these all the time."

Without asking, the boys bounded up the steps, and Ernestine could hear them going through the cabinets, opening the bathroom door, the microwave. Jumping on the bed. Fiddling with the TV.

"Hey look at this," one of them hollered. "This is so rad."

"Oh man," the other one hollered back, "I could totally live in this."

"Yeah, totally."

The term "geezer mobile" struck a sour note with Ernestine. "What kind of rude talk is that?" she said. "Calling their grandparents geezers?"

"Mom, don't get your back up," Linda said. "It's just an expression."

Linda's husband, Matt, a cop with the California Highway Patrol, worked nights and slept during the day. It was early for him to be getting up, but all the commotion in the driveway woke him and he came out of the house finger-combing his hair. "Hey there, Walt," he said, shaking Walter's hand. "Good to see you."

He turned to Ernestine, "Hi, Mom. The hair's new, isn't it?"

"My hairdresser talked me into it. What do you think?"

"Looks good." He gave Ernestine a hug and turned his attention to the motorhome. "Awfully big investment at your age."

21

Clearly insulted, Walter said, "I don't see what my age has to do with it."

"How does it handle? Any trouble coming over that Elkhorn Bridge?"

"No problem at all. Just like driving my pickup."

"Well, she's a beauty all right. I see the boys've inspected it already. I'll take a look after I have a cup of coffee. But you need to move her. Park down on the street so I can get my car out. I have to go to work tonight."

Matt went back in the house, and Ernestine, bristling from the unpleasant beginning, followed him in. Walter hoisted himself up into the cab and started the engine. "You boys have to sit down now, while we're moving."

He idled for a minute, checking the mirrors. He had never backed it up before, and it was sitting at an awkward angle on the steep driveway. He released the brake and eased backward.

"Grampa, stop!" Jack yelled. "The wa—" There was a ripping, wrenching sound. The concrete block wall between Linda and Matt's yard and the next-door neighbors' was in Walter's blind spot.

"Holy crap!" Jeremy said. "Gramma's gonna kill you."

The noise brought everybody running. Linda, Matt, Ernestine, the neighbors.

Walter pulled forward, climbed down, and walked around to see the damage. "Oops," he said, looking sheepish. A deep crease ran about ten feet along the side from in front of the rear wheel all the way through the passenger door, which was now swinging open.

"Oops?" Ernestine squealed. "OOPS? That's all you can say, Walter? Look what you've done. It's practically ruined."

"No, it's not ruined. Quit fussing. It's only a scratch, and I can fix the door. It was bound to happen sooner or later, so now we don't have to worry about it." He climbed back into the driver's seat, pulled forward to adjust his angle, backed into the street, and parked.

During dinner, while Ernestine stewed over the damage, Walter held court telling the boys about trips he'd taken when he was their age, most of which Ernestine suspected had never happened.

When the dishes were cleared, Linda brought out a birthday cake and Walter opened his gifts. There was a fly rod from Linda and Matt, and a fly-making kit from the boys. "We thought you needed a hobby," Linda said. "We didn't know you were buying a motorhome."

Later when Ernestine and Linda stood on the front steps watching Walter pound on the hinges to get the damaged door to close, Linda said, "You know this is a bad idea, don't you? Matt says he sees wrecks all the time involving old people with motorhomes. And look what Dad's done to it already."

Ernestine stiffened. Why did Linda have to keep bringing up their ages?

"Are you sure Dad's okay driving that thing? I think you're crazy to be doing this. How is he going to back it into tight spaces in RV parks if he can't even back out of our driveway?"

The lecture was aggravating. Admittedly, Walter had made a mess of things. The long scrape on the side and the bent-up door made the motorhome look like it had been in a wreck. But Walter had his heart set on this trip and Ernestine wasn't going to let Linda ruin it for him.

"Your father can drive as well as he ever did. He's just not used to the motorhome yet."

"How about you?"

"What about me?"

"Can you drive it? If something happens to him?"

"Nothing is going to happen to him."

Linda walked to the edge of the porch, stood there with her back to Ernestine for a few minutes, and then retraced her steps. "Well, it's pretty clear you're not going to listen to reason. So I have to ask, are you prepared for emergencies?"

"Your dad has everything under control."

"What does that mean?"

"Your Uncle Richard showed him how to operate everything, and he has a whole stack of Good Sam magazines with all kinds of information."

"Do you have a cell phone?"

"No we don't. We've never needed one."

"Well you need one now. What if you run out of gas or need towing? What if someone tries to rob you? What if something does happen to Dad?"

Ernestine took a deep breath and let it out. "Okay, okay. I see what you mean."

"We'll get you a phone tomorrow."

"You're going to have to talk your dad into it. You know how he is about technology."

Thirteen-year-old Jeremy, who'd been listening to the conversation between his mom and grandma, piped up. "Wait, I know! They can have my old phone. It works, all except for the camera. Then I can get a new one."

Linda frowned at Jeremy, thought for a moment, and then nodded. "Actually, that's not a bad idea. Maybe we can get the camera fixed. What's wrong with it?"

"Nothing bad. Just there's dust or something inside so there's squiggles on all the pictures."

5

The next morning Linda presented her plan to Walter.

"No," he said. "We don't need a cell phone. We've been fine without one all this time."

"Yes, Dad, but you've been home with a land line until now."

"Damn things are expensive. We can use phone booths if we need to call anyone."

"Dad, where've you been? You can't even find a phone booth anymore. I'll put you on my plan and the phone won't cost you anything. You won't have to worry about it."

When they got to the Apple store, Linda checked in to the Genius Bar. "We have a limited number of walk-in appointments," the girl said. "I'll put you on the list, but it'll be a bit of a wait."

The place was packed with young people wearing ripped skinny jeans, baggy shirts, and thick rimmed glasses, milling around tables displaying laptop computers, or just standing looking down at their phones. The bright lights were giving Ernestine a headache, and Walter kept making remarks about the "kids in blue shirts who must work here but don't look busy." Within ten minutes he was twitching with impatience.

"I've signed us up to see a Genius," Linda said, "but it'll be a bit of a wait."

"To see a what?" Walter asked.

"A customer service rep. They call them Geniuses."

"What arrogance. Let's go."

"No, Dad," Linda said. "This is important. You and mom are going to be driving all over the country. I need to have a way to reach you."

"You said the phone works."

"Yes, but it has Jeremy's phone number. We need to get you guys your own number. And I want to see if they can fix the camera."

"I thought you said it was a phone."

"Yes, but it's also a camera."

"Your mom has a camera."

"But it's not digital, Dad. The iPhone camera is digital. You don't need to buy film. You don't have to get the pictures developed, and you can see them right away."

"Bah."

"Dad, you're going to national parks. Mom's going to want to take pictures."

"Okay, okay, but we don't have all day to wait around." Walter shoved his hands in his pockets and paced.

While they were waiting, Linda questioned Ernestine. "How long do you plan to be gone?"

"We haven't decided."

"What about money? I hope you're not carrying a lot of cash."

"No, I know better than that. I've got a credit card."

"How did you get Dad to agree to that? I know how he feels about credit cards."

"I just did it."

"And your mail? What are you doing about your mail?"

"Mavis, next door. She's going to pick it up. I'll call her and she'll tell me if there's anything important."

"I don't know, Mom. This is insane."

"Linda, I'm your mother. You don't need to treat me like a child!"

"Well, excuse me!" Linda turned and walked to where Walter and Jeremy were examining one of the newest iPads.

After a long wait a voice called, "Linda Wright?"

"It's about time," Walter said, noting that the "Genius" didn't look much older than Jeremy's fifteen-year-old brother Jack. His dark hair was combed up in a peak, he had earrings in both ears, and a white iPhone hung around his neck on a lanyard.

"My name is Devon," he crooned, "What can I help you with?"

Linda handed him the phone. "We're giving this to my parents, so it needs to be set up for them."

"Not a problem."

"And, while you're at it, there's a issue with the camera. It works, but there are flecks or hairs inside that leave marks on the pictures."

Devon snapped a picture and looked at the phone. "I totally see what you're saying." His voice oozed empathy. "It can definitely be fixed, but unfortunately we'll have to send it—"

"Send it, my ass," Walter's voice bounced off the room's hard surfaces. "We don't have time to send it anywhere. Forget about the camera. Just give us a number."

Back in Linda's Suburban, the boys started explaining how to use the iPhone. "Everything is right on this screen—see. Just a quick swipe of the finger—here, Grandma, you try."

Ernestine started pushing the icons.

"No, don't push, just tap, like this." Jack and Jeremy, both talking at once, showed her the "really awesome apps," the "really cool games," where to find her phone number, how to put in her own contacts, and how Linda's number was already programmed in. They showed her how to use the camera and how to buy things on the internet.

Ernestine nodded, not getting any of it.

At Linda's insistence, they stopped at what she called a "cute little restaurant" for lunch where the service was so slow that Walter kept getting up and trying to leave.

Linda's repeated, "sit down, Dad" seemed to agitate him even more and by the time they got their food Ernestine was ready to choke him.

"Are you sure this trip is Dad's idea?" Linda said on their way to the car. "He seems crankier than usual."

"Of course it's his idea," Ernestine snapped. "And you're right, he is cranky."

It was nearly two o'clock when they got back to the house and Matt was getting up for his shift. He came out of the bedroom to say goodbye and asked, "Where're you headed first?"

"Yosemite," Walter said. "Should've been halfway there by now. Damn cell phone business took up the whole day."

"Do you have a reservation?"

"No, but the Good Sam book says you can get a place outside the park. First come, first serve."

"Good luck with that," Matt said. "I read somewhere that the park had over four million visitors last year. I hope you have an alternate plan."

"Well," Walter said, "we'll just have to see."

"Don't forget to call," Linda hollered as they drove off. "Let us know where you are."

As soon as they were out of Linda's sight, Walter pointed to the Good Sam Directory and told Ernestine to call and see if she could get them a space. She fiddled with the phone for several minutes before giving up. Even after having been drilled by the boys, she couldn't make it work. Walter pulled onto Highway 99 and headed south, mumbling about all the time they had wasted on that useless cell phone.

6

We're in luck," Walter crowed when he came back from the RV office. "There are two pull-through sites left and they have everything we need, including full hookups and Wi-Fi, whatever that is. They even gave us a senior discount." He handed Ernestine some pamphlets the park manager gave him, studied the campground map, located number 46, pulled in between two big rigs about the same size as the Allegro, and climbed down to assess the situation. His brother-in-law, Richard, had emphasized the importance of leveling the rig to enable the refrigerator to function properly.

"Besides which," Richard had said, "you don't want to be sleeping with your feet higher than your head or have the eggs roll off the counter when you're making breakfast."

Walter opened up the RV's side compartment and removed the leveling blocks, electrical cords, and hoses, all the while hoping the owners of the rigs on either side were absent so he wouldn't be seen as a greenhorn. He placed the blocks against the tires, then got back in, started the engine, and released the parking brake. The trick, Richard had said, was to allow the engine to idle as you gave it just enough gas to power the unit up the ramp of blocks.

Every time Walter tried it, he went up and over the blocks. And every time that happened, he blamed Ernestine for not telling him to stop soon enough. After five or six tries, the rig was up on two of the blocks and only slightly catawampus.

"Close enough," he said. It was getting dark and he still had the hookups to do. "Help me here," he said pulling the big anaconda-like sewer hose away from the rig. "I need you to hold this so I can attach the hose clamp and tighten the—" On the third try, he pinched his finger and started to swear. By this time Ernestine was fuming. He was acting like it was her fault he was having trouble. Besides, she was hungry and wanted to get in the motorhome and start supper.

"First time?"

Walter looked up to see a tall, well-built man in a tank top and Speedo swim suit stepping out of the motorhome six feet away.

"Please. I would like to help you." The man said holding out his hand. "I am called André. What do they call you?"

Detecting an accent, Walter slowed his own speech. "I'm Wal-ter and this is my wife, Er-nes-tine. It's our first time out. I'm em-barrassed."

"Don't be. Somewhere we all have to start," André walked over to his own motorhome and pounded on the door. "Fifi, come out. Meet our new neighbors."

A skinny woman with short yellow hair and skin that looked like an old saddle opened the door and balanced herself on the retractable steps. She held a glass of red wine and a cigarette.

Making a grand motion toward the two newcomers, André said, "Fifi, meet Walter and Ernestine."

"The name's Frances," she said, flicking the ashes off the end of her cigarette. "André's French. He's the only one that calls me Fifi. Where you from?"

"A ways north of here," Walter offered. "Say, I need to get cracking on setting this thing up."

While the men worked on the hoses and the power cords, Fifi and Ernestine sat at the picnic table between the two RVs. Fifi brought out a box of red wine and two glasses, and Ernestine, feeling called upon to be social, stepped into her RV and got the rice crackers and hummus she'd bought at Trader Joe's.

Fifi turned out to be so talkative that Ernestine didn't need to say anything. She couldn't go in and fix the tacos she'd planned for supper until the men got everything hooked up, so she sat, accepting glass after glass of wine, and listening to Fifi talk.

"I'm from Cleveland," Fifi confided. "I met André years ago when I was in Paris with some girlfriends.

Back then, we were all hot for Frenchmen because we'd heard how sexy they are, you know, and romantic, and how they love American women. And it's true. At least it's true of André. He's very sexy, and very adventurous in sex."

Ernestine blushed and hoped Fifi wasn't going to tell her how adventurous. She'd already gathered from André's tank top with the chest hair sprouting in all directions, and his skin-tight spandex shorts, that he was way sexier than, say, Walter.

"On the other hand," Fifi went on, oblivious to Ernestine's red face, "they also tend to stray, if you know what I mean. I have to keep a tight rein on my André."

Ernestine, feeling the effects of the wine, and afraid of where this conversation was going, wanted to change the subject, but her head had begun to spin. The Allegro's slide outs were open and it looked like the hookup was done, but the men were still talking. Walter, gesturing with his hands, appeared to be explaining how the damage on the side of the motorhome had happened. Ernestine thought about joining them but she was afraid she would tip over if she stood up. When Walter came to get her, she wasn't in any shape to cook supper, and if the motorhome was a little bit off kilter, she didn't notice.

7

The next morning Ernestine rose early. She denied she'd had too much to drink and, although she couldn't remember cooking dinner the night before, she was sure she had. She went all out fixing eggs and pancakes, enjoying her new electric griddle and her colorful plastic dishes. Even making the coffee was fun with the tiny four-cup Mr. Coffee machine. She had never done bacon in a microwave before, so had no idea how quickly it would cook. Before she knew it, smoke was billowing out of the little appliance, filling the space with the acrid smell of burnt bacon. She opened the windows and turned on the fan over the stove, but even so, the smell and smoke hung in the air.

It was after ten when she stepped out into the sunshine and was surprised to see that André and Fifi's rig was gone. In its place was a small travel trailer, the kind Ernestine had dismissed as undesirable.

"Hi there," A young girl called from the table where Ernestine had spent the previous evening.

"Oh," Ernestine said, taking in the girl's tattoo-covered cleavage and upper arms, "I was expecting someone else."

Just then a tall young man stepped out of the trailer. He was covered with tattoos as well, but what Ernestine found most shocking was all the metal things hanging from his nose, ears, and lips. "Mornin," he said, coming around the table to shake her hand. "We came in last night. Guess you were sleepin'."

"Oh, I see," Ernestine stammered, "will you excuse me just a moment? My husband's inside. I'll get him so he can say hello." She stepped back in and closed the door. "Walter," she whispered, "we have new neighbors and you need to be nice."

"Why's that?"

"Because you're going to have opinions."

He went to the window and looked out. "Good Lord, that kid's head looks like a tackle box."

"Yes, I know, but we can't judge people by their looks."

"The hell we can't."

"Walter, we just started this trip and we're going to be meeting all kinds of people. I'm sure he's perfectly nice. Come out and say hello. And don't be rude."

Mumbling under his breath, he followed Ernestine out and extended his hand. "Name's Walter. Pleased to meet you."

"Mike," the young man said, shaking Walter's hand. "And that's Sherry."

Walter nodded at the girl, then turned and started to unplug the cord from the power pole.

"You headin' out?" Mike asked.

Walter looked sideways at the kid. "No, we'll stay one more night. Right now, though, we're going to go drive through the park."

"Bad idea, man. Big rigs like yours just tie up traffic. It's better to leave it here and catch the shuttle from the visitor center." He pointed up the road. "Just a short walk. The bus'll take you on the whole loop through the park and you'll see everything."

Looking surprised by the practical advice, Walter mumbled, "Oh, well, thanks. I didn't know about that."

Walter and Ernestine were both out of breath by the time they reached the visitor center where there was a long line of tourists, most of them carrying cameras. Looking around, Ernestine noticed people of various ethnicities and tried to identify the different languages she heard. When it was their turn to board, the only seats left were singles near the rear of the bus. Walter sat down by an overweight woman with a huge straw hat, and Ernestine took a seat across the aisle next to a teenage boy who was typing with his thumbs on a gadget that looked a lot like her new iPhone.

"Hi there," she said, turning to the boy. He ignored her, so she leaned forward and over a bit. "Hi," she said again. "Is that a cell phone? What's that you're doing with it?"

"Eh, yeah. I'm texting."

"Texting? What's that?"

"You know." He looked over and, seeing that she was an old lady, said, "Well, it's like talking on the phone, only without talking."

"Oh, talking without talking. How does that work?"

"I type and my friend types back."

"On those tiny little keys? And you seem to be going so fast."

"Uh huh. I, like, use a lot of shortcuts."

"Shortcuts? Like what?"

"You know, abbreviations. Like if something is funny, I type LOL for laugh out loud. Or if it's really funny, ROTFL for rolling on the floor laughing."

"I see. Do you suppose you could help me with something?" Ernestine opened her pocketbook and took out the iPhone. "We just got this and I can't seem to make it work."

The boy looked surprised. "Well sure, I guess, but didn't they give you any instructions?"

"Yes, my grandsons showed me how to use it, but I can't remember what I'm supposed to do. I want to call my daughter. Could you—?"

The kid took the phone, found the number, and pressed "call."

When Linda picked up, Ernestine glanced at the kid and smiled.

"How's Dad?" Linda asked.

"He's fine, and since you didn't ask, so am I."

"Sorry," Linda said. "How's it going? Where are you now?"

Ernestine told her they had camped the night before and were on a shuttle bus that would be taking them through Yosemite National Park, and that a nice young man had helped her make the phone call. "I just want to let you know where we are, but I have to sign off now because we are coming into the park and I am going to have my young friend here show me how to take pictures with this gadget."

Ernestine, nearly breathless over the scenery, could do little but ooh and aah at the giant sequoia trees, the spray from the waterfalls, and the way the light lit up the massive rock faces. Using the brochure from the visitor center, she identified each feature as they came to it, the Half Dome, El Capitan, Yosemite Falls, and took pictures of each one with her phone.

Back at the campsite, there was something else to take pictures of. The Allegro had been knocked off the leveling blocks, the driver's side was scratched and clawed, and the kitchen window hung loose from its casing.

"Bear," Mike said when they walked up. "Big damn bear. I seen him over there rocking yer rig back and forth. Thought he was going to tip it over."

Ernestine was aghast. "Why didn't you do something? Couldn't you scare him off? Make him stop?"

"You kiddin' me? I stayed in my rig. Wasn't about to come out here."

Ernestine was beside herself. Now the RV not only had a huge crease on the passenger side, but the driver's side looked like shit too.

"Didn't you read the warnings about bears?" Mike asked. "You left the windows open and I could smell bacon."

Just as he had when he'd run into the wall at Linda's, Walter seemed unperturbed. Without saying a word, he went inside for the brochures he'd been given when they first arrived. Sure enough, it was there in bold letters: KEEP FOOD OUT OF SIGHT. KEEP WINDOWS, VENTS, AND DOORS CLOSED WHEN YOU ARE NOT THERE. BEARS CAN EASILY RIP THE WINDOW OUT OF A CAR DOOR. Ernestine conceded it was her fault for not reading the warnings and for going off without closing the windows, but it annoyed her that Walter wasn't as upset about the damage as she was.

Still fuming, she went inside to attend to chores, one of which was caring for the cat. Even though Vivian was Walter's pet, it had somehow become her job to clean the litter box and set out food and water. Opening a can of Fancy Feast, she called, "Kitty, Kitty, Kitty," and when Vivian didn't appear, she walked to the back of the motorhome. When they weren't on the road, Vivian usually slept on Walter's pillow, but she wasn't there. Puzzled, Ernestine stuck her head into the tiny bathroom where she kept the litter pan. No Vivian.

"Walter," she called, "have you seen the cat?"

"No, did you check the bed? That's where she likes to sleep."

"I know where she likes to sleep. Of course I checked the bed."

Walter put down the pamphlet he was reading and helped her look. Vivian wasn't under the bed, or in the clothes closet, or behind the curtains. She wasn't under the sofa and she wasn't in the cabinet under the sink.

"Oh my God, Walter. The window was open. She was probably scared to death and ran." Bumping into each other, they both headed for the door.

"Mike, Sherry," Walter hollered, pounding on the side of the rusty RV.

Mike opened the door. "What's up, man?" He didn't have a shirt on and Ernestine noticed how odd his white un-tattooed chest looked next to his colorful arms.

"Have you seen a cat? Calico. Black patch over one eye, orange over the other?"

"Nope. You're traveling with a cat?"

"Yes, but she's gone. Must have climbed out that window. Keep an eye out, will you?"

Walter and Ernestine headed in opposite directions, knocking on the doors of neighboring campers, asking if they'd seen a cat. No one had. Ernestine felt terrible. She was the one who had ignored the warning about the bears. She was the one who had burnt the bacon. She was the one who left the window open to clear out the smoke.

They searched for over an hour, looking under trailers and up in trees, before giving up and going back inside. "Walter, I'm so sorry," Ernestine said. "I know how fond you are of that cat and it's my fault she's gone."

"Let's stick around for another day or two," Walter said. "I think she'll find her way back."

8

Ernestine fixed supper, but the fun had gone out of it. She was nervous about cooking anything that might give off a smell. Frying hamburgers was out, as was grilling the nice pre-marinated steaks she'd brought along. She didn't want any odors to escape, so while potatoes baked in the little gas oven, she got out a roll of aluminum foil and some duct tape and made Walter patch the opening where the window had been.

Sleep didn't come easy. She couldn't stop thinking about Vivian being out there somewhere. Couldn't help thinking about bears. And about what a bear might do to a cat. Her only comfort was knowing cats can climb trees. But so can bears.

She'd almost fallen asleep, when she heard a loud racket. "Walter!" She nudged his shoulder. "Walter, wake up!"

"What?"

"Something's out there." She grabbed her robe and made her way to the front where they'd drawn a curtain across the windshield. Crouching between the two seats, she opened it just enough to peer out. A light illuminated the enclosed area where the garbage cans were, and sure enough, an enormous brown bear was standing on his hind legs digging through the cans, strewing a wide swath of trash. Badly shaken, she went back to the bed. "Walter, it *was* a bear. Maybe the same one. I'm sorry about Vivian, but I don't want to stay here any longer than we have to."

Early the next morning while Walter went about getting the sewer pipe and the water hose unhooked and stowed away, Ernestine went over to Mike and Sherry's RV and handed them a piece of paper with her cell phone number on it. "I'm not sure where we'll be," she said, "but please call me if the cat comes back."

Once Walter had everything put away and had closed up the slide outs, he drove off the leveling blocks, got out, picked them up, and waved to Sherry and Mike who were watching from the picnic table. He'd driven about five feet when the rig lurched and stalled.

"The power cord," Ernestine said, "did you disconnect it?"

Walter got out and walked around the rig. "I'm learning," he said to Mike who was grinning and wagging his finger. "I'll get it figured out."

It was only their third day in the motorhome, but Ernestine had already figured out a couple of things. Number one, she needed to read all the brochures and make sure she knew what to expect. And number two, Walter was not as sure of himself as he had led her to believe.

Leaving the campground, it occurred to her that there might be an animal shelter nearby. "If Vivian turns up, they could let us know."

"You can give it a try," Walter said, "But how will you find a phone number?"

She held up the cell phone. "I'll call information." She pushed the on button and nothing happened. She tried again. Nothing. "Dang it," she said, remembering what Jeremy told her about charging the battery. She got up and went to the back and rummaged through her luggage looking for the cord. "I'll try later," she said plugging the phone into the port in the RV's console.

Walter pulled out onto the highway. "Let's take that Tioga Pass road," he said. "From there we can connect with U.S. 395. That's supposed to be the most scenic route to Death Valley."

Preoccupied with the latest damage to the RV and how it had led to the loss of the cat, Ernestine just nodded. Every few minutes she checked the phone to see if it was done charging and when it was, she dialed 411 and got a number for the local animal shelter.

No one had turned in a cat with Vivian's description, but the woman she spoke to, took her information and agreed to let her know if the cat showed up. "Well,"

Ernestine said when she ended the call. "I guess that's all we can do."

With that done, she turned her attention to the road and realized she should have been paying attention. There were extreme drop-offs on both sides and Walter kept veering closer and closer to the edge. The fog was rolling in, too, and the higher they got the harder it was to see. Ernestine grabbed the strap above her window and held on. When they reached the 9,943 foot summit and started downhill, she could feel they were going too fast. "For the love of God Walter," she said, "slow down. You're going to get us killed." That's when she noticed he was frantically pumping the brake pedal. She looked at his face. He was gritting his teeth.

"What is it? What's wrong?"

"The brakes."

"What?"

"The brakes. They feel spongy."

"What do you mean spongy? We don't have brakes?"

"Hold on," Walter said cutting her off, "I'm taking..."

When they hit the gravel in the runaway truck ramp, Ernestine thought she was going to faint. They slid for a long ways, and when the RV finally came to a stop, she and Walter sat and stared at each other. His hat had flown off and her red hair was standing straight up.

"That was quick thinking," the highway patrolman who pulled up behind them said. "At the speed you were going, you'd have gone over the edge for sure. I'm going to radio ahead for a tow truck and notify the highway department. Tow truck'll take you into Lee

Vining. There's a brake shop there. You might be sitting here awhile, though. You folks gonna be okay?"

Still in shock, Ernestine could only nod. Walter seemed to have swallowed his tongue as well.

After the patrolman left, Ernestine moved from the front seat to the sofa and put her head in her hands. Her insides felt all wobbly from the fright and she wondered if what just happened was Walter's fault. Was he going too fast because the brakes had failed? Or did the brakes fail because he was going too fast? She didn't know. But thank God he'd had the presence of mind to employ the ramp.

The tow truck was taking forever. It was getting dark and they were both hungry. Digging through their provisions, Ernestine made sandwiches and opened a bag of chips. She was tempted to pour them each a glass of wine, but thought better of it. It could complicate the situation, she reasoned, if Walter had alcohol on his breath.

The tow truck showed up just as they finished eating. "You have triple A?" the bearded driver asked. "I gotta see your card."

Ernestine found it in her pocketbook and handed it over.

"Hmm," the driver said, "you're in luck. Your plan covers towing up to a hundred miles, so we're okay on that." He jotted down the information from the card, then asked to see Walter's driver's license. "You folks'll have to ride with me. Can't have you in the rig whilst I tow it."

Ernestine watched the man, who seemed way too old to be doing this job, hook the wench to the back of the motorhome and secure it to his truck. "We need to pull her out of this ramp," he said, signaling for Walter and Ernestine to climb up into his truck. Walter got in first, scooted to the middle and straddled the gearshift. Ernestine squeezed in between him and the door. The cab was littered with fast food boxes and pop cans and smelled revolting.

At the top of the escape ramp, the driver stopped. "You folks sit tight. I gotta switch things around." He ran the wench again, lowering the Allegro to the ground, got out, unhooked the motorhome, and got back in the cab. Before Ernestine could ask what was happening, he pulled in front of the rig, jumped back out and reattached the motorhome.

Impressed with his efficiency, she said, "You must have done this before."

"E-yup." It was more of a grunt than an answer. Walter had gone mute and the driver didn't seem to welcome conversation, so in the relative silence of the tow truck, Ernestine conjured up all sorts of misgivings about continuing the trip. She couldn't get Linda's remarks about accidents involving elderly people in motorhomes out of her mind. And she wondered why she had agreed to take this trip in the first place.

The tow truck driver pulled into the lot at Jake's Brake Shop in Lee Vining. "They'll take care of you here," he said hopping down from his seat. While he unhooked the motorhome, Ernestine climbed down out of the truck and waited for Walter to do the same. He got out but just stood staring at the front end of the Allegro.

"Walter," she said, nudging him, "let's go inside." He didn't move. Annoyed, she crossed the parking lot without him and entered the office. The woman at the desk looked up and Ernestine pointed out the window. "That's our motorhome out there. The brakes went out coming down the mountain."

"Oh mercy," the woman said. "That must have been frightening."

"It most certainly was."

"I'll send Jake out. He'll take a look at it."

The fellow in the greasy coveralls introduced himself as Jake, and Walter, coming out of his stupor, started explaining. "I was coming down that Tioga Road there and the brakes went all spongy on me. Pedal went all the way to the floor."

"How'd you get 'er stopped?"

"Don't know. Got lucky I guess."

"Wow. Sounds like you lost your brake fluid. That can happen with these big rigs. It's a pretty easy fix though. Replace the brake line and the brake fluid. I gotta say, you were damn lucky, you and your missus. Damn lucky. Tell you what, I can't get to it till tomorrow, but you're welcome to plug yer rig into my electricity. Stay here tonight."

"That's awfully nice of you," Ernestine said, "Awfully nice."

9

The brake job was finished by mid-afternoon the next day, and Walter, anxious to get to Death Valley, pulled onto Hwy 395. The Good Sam book listed campgrounds called Furnace Creek and Stovepipe Wells, making what Ernestine had heard about Death Valley feel all the more ominous. The book also said space was limited, so now that the iPhone was charged, Ernestine called Stovepipe Wells and was told there were no vacancies. Next she called Furnace Creek, only to find out that they required four days' advance notice.

"Well?" Walter said, glancing at her. "What did they say?"

"They said we have to give four days' notice and it's only a day's drive from here."

"We'll just go. If we show up, they'll have to let us stay."

"No, they won't have to let us stay," Ernestine said. "We'll be down there and we won't have any place to park this thing."

"We're going. We'll just have to see."

As Walter drove, Ernestine read to him from the Good Sam book. "Death Valley is the hottest, driest place in North America. Between 1931 and 1934, there was a forty-month period with only 0.64 inches of rain."

Walter nodded.

"And the highest ground temperature ever recorded, 134°F, was at Furnace Creek. That was in July of 1913." This alarmed her. "I had no idea it could get that hot."

Walter nodded again.

"That was at Furnace Creek, Walter. Where we're going."

"This isn't 1913."

"But it *is* July."

"That's why we have the air conditioner. We'll be fine."

Ernestine read to herself and tried not to think what she was thinking. "We don't have enough drinking water," she said after a while. "It says here we need a gallon a day for each of us. And we need to watch for signs of heat stroke. And we have to be careful where we put our hands and feet because there are snakes and scorpions and black widow spiders. Walter, this isn't a good idea."

"We'll be inside, with air conditioning. And we'll watch where we put our hands and feet. Okay?"

"I don't understand you. Why are you so unconcerned? You're the one who's afraid of spiders. You're the one who'll be sticking your hands into small openings."

He kept driving like nothing she was telling him made any difference.

"Have you been listening to me? There are spiders and scorpions and 130-degree temperatures, this is crazy. Why are you still driving?"

"Because I want to see Death Valley. So let's just do it."

The drive was going to be just over four hours, five if Ernestine could get him to stop for water. But even though she disagreed about the owners of the camp letting them stay without a reservation, she decided to keep her mouth shut and let him find out for himself. If worse came to worst, she supposed they could pull off somewhere and sleep.

She had hoped the drive would be scenic, but it was all dry dirt and distant hills. She would have turned on the radio, but Walter never liked music when he drove. He said he needed to listen to the engine. Watching the road made her sleepy. Her eyelids felt heavy. Every few minutes her head would drop, startling her awake.

"Go ahead and sleep," Walter said. "You don't need to watch me drive."

That was just it. She considered it her job to watch him drive. What if he got sleepy too? What if there was something in the road he didn't see? What if he missed a turn? The engine droned on, and she fought to keep her eyes open.

There wasn't anyone in the little kiosk when they drove into the campground at around 8:30 p.m.

"What'll we do?" Ernestine asked. "No one's here to take our money."

It wasn't quite dark, so they could see that many of the spaces were empty. Walter idled the engine and chewed on his upper lip. "Let's just find us a place and worry about it in the morning?" Ernestine didn't like doing things that way, it didn't seem right. On the other hand, she didn't want to go looking for some other place either.

Putting the gearshift in drive, Walter eased over what looked like a cattle guard and into the park. He passed seven or eight empty spaces before he decided to pull into one. It had all the hookups and wasn't so near the entrance that they'd be noticed right away.

"What do you think?" he asked.

Ernestine shrugged. "I guess all they can do is run us out."

Walter stayed behind the wheel and she climbed down from the rig, intending to help by positioning the leveling blocks. Before she had a chance to get them from the storage compartment, she heard errrr, errrr, errrr, and the motorhome began lifting on its own. First one side, then the other, until it was level.

"What'd you just do?" she asked when he stepped down to join her.

"Leveling jacks. I forgot all about them."

"For God's sake, Walter, you put me through all that with the blocks and we could have leveled it with jacks all this time?" She went inside. She would have slammed the door, but there was no point, because it

53

only made a squishing noise instead of a bang. What was the matter with him anyway?

When he finished getting everything hooked up, Walter came back inside. Ernestine had set the table and placed a big salad in the middle of it.

"Is that what we're having for dinner?"

"Yes. I don't want to use the stove."

"And why's that?"

"Because of bears. I don't want any smells escaping."

"They don't have bears in Death Valley."

"There's other things, though. Coyotes, foxes, not to mention snakes and spiders and scorpions."

"Coyotes and foxes aren't going to break in the windows like the bear did."

"You don't know that."

Walter started to argue but seeming to change his mind, sat down and ate the salad.

That night they both had trouble falling asleep. Walter because of the heat, and Ernestine because she kept thinking she felt things crawling on her. She woke to the smell of coffee. Walter was in the kitchen stirring a bowl of pancake batter. "Good morning," he said. "Thought I'd get us a good start before we go take a look at this place."

Surprised by his perkiness, Ernestine poured herself a cup of coffee and looked out the window. "Pretty darn desolate, if you ask me. I wonder what there is to see."

"Well let's walk down to that kiosk and see if we can find somebody to pay. Explain that we came in late. I'm sure they'll let us stay since there aren't many people here."

"What time is it anyhow? Seems awful early to be so hot."

"Quarter past six," he said. "And I'd guess it's almost eighty degrees already."

While they ate breakfast, Walter listed some things he wanted to see. The Harmony Borax Works was one of them, and Scotty's Castle, and he wanted to see some of the old mines he'd heard about. But that would be tomorrow. Today he just wanted to get out and look around. "Get some clothes on," he said, "we need to explore this place before it gets too dang hot."

In spite of the heat, Ernestine put on jeans and closed-toed shoes. Shorts and sandals would have felt better, but she didn't know what kind of creatures were out there. In fact, she wished she'd brought a pair of sturdy hiking boots. She put a long-sleeved shirt over her tee, covered her face and neck with sunscreen, and donned a wide-brimmed hat.

"Good grief," Walter said when she stepped outside, "you're going to cook in that get-up." He was wearing shorts, a t-shirt, and open-toed sandals. He wasn't even wearing a cap.

"Maybe so," Ernestine said, "but I'd rather have heat stroke than die from a snake bite."

The kiosk was quite a ways back from where they'd camped. Walter strutted like a rooster, looking happy to be out of the confines of the RV and able to stretch his legs. Ernestine, on the other hand, plodded along with her head down, examining the ground for snakes, or worse, scorpions. Each time they passed an occupied campsite, Walter commented about no one else being up and around. "Hot weather must make people lazy."

Ernestine didn't see any of the dreaded snakes or scorpions, but looking as intently as she was, she became fascinated with the patterns that had formed in the dry, cracked soil. She kept trying to find words to describe what she saw. Some of it looked like leather. Some like broken tiles. In some places the wind had blown sand into undulating hills that the sun lit up in such a way that made her catch her breath. It wasn't ugly like she'd thought at first. It was just so different, with a unique beauty all its own. She reached into her pocket for the cell phone. Even if the pictures ended up having that squiggle across them, she had to capture what she saw. Everywhere she looked there was something interesting. The yellow mud, the steep-walled gullies, low mesquite shrubs, and gnarled trees, their shapes bizarre and yet somehow human. She'd crouched down to get a good angle on a cactus plant when she realized Walter was standing beside her.

"Here, give me a hand will you?"

"For God's sake, Ernie, you scared me."

She looked at his face, he looked stricken. "What's wrong?"

He pulled her to her feet. "I thought you'd had heat stroke. All those clothes and you down on the ground like that."

"Oh, Walter," she said, putting her hand on his cheek, "I'm sorry I scared you. I'm fine. I got down here to take this picture and I couldn't get up. I guess I'm too old to be a nature photographer." She tucked her arm in his and they walked to the kiosk.

No one was there this time either, but there was a notice beside a box of envelopes saying to deposit your check through a slot.

"Do you have a check with you," Walter asked.

She shook her head.

"Oh well," he said. "I'll walk back here later and take care of it. See, it's like I told you. No problem."

The sun was higher in the sky now and Ernestine was beginning to feel light headed. Once they were back inside the RV, though, the cool air felt heavenly. She took off her hat and her over-shirt, changed into shorts, and was reaching into the refrigerator for bottles of cold water when a high-pitched screeching noise, like metal against metal, started. "What on earth?" She covered her ears. "What is that?"

Walter was as alarmed as she was. He jumped up and rushed out the door. A man from a neighboring campsite was standing about ten feet away from the Allegro looking concerned.

"Did you hear that?" Walter asked.

"Sure did."

"Any idea what it is?"

"Yeah, I do. Happened to me once. It's your AC."

"The air conditioner? No. That wouldn't be good."

"Check it out. See if it's running."

Just then Ernestine stuck her head out the door. "Walter, the air went off."

"What'd you have it set at?" the man asked.

"Sixty-eight. Like at home."

"There's your problem. Its 115 degrees right now and you can only expect them things to cool down about twenty degrees from that. You'll have to go to Vegas to get it fixed. There's no place around here."

Walter thanked the man and went inside. "There's so much I wanted to see," he said.

"I'm sorry," Ernestine said, "but it's so hot. We can't stay here without air conditioning."

Sweating profusely, Walter unhooked and stowed the cords and hoses. They managed to leave the campsite without incident, and Ernestine, though faulting him for his lack of foresight—coming to the hottest place on the face of the earth in July—recognized that he had gotten better at setting up and taking down. And, to be honest, she was relieved to be leaving Death Valley.

They went a long way without speaking, but when Ernestine saw a sign that read Funeral Mountain Wilderness, she couldn't resist pointing it out. "It's an omen, Walter. We weren't supposed to stay here."

"Maybe you're right," he sighed, glancing in the rearview mirror. "Maybe you're right."

At Death Valley Junction they picked up CA 127 and headed for Las Vegas. Ernestine followed the lines on the map with her finger and tried to tell Walter which roads to take, but he wasn't listening. They approached a sign pointing to Pahrump, and she signaled for him to turn, but he ignored her. According to her calculations, he was going the wrong way, but not wanting to needle him, she decided to let him figure it out.

"Maybe Las Vegas will be cooler," she said.

Walter mopped his forehead. "Even if it is, I doubt we'll be able to tell the difference."

10

About twenty miles beyond the Pahrump turnoff, Walter veered onto a gravel road.

"What are you doing?" Ernestine asked.

"I think I should have taken that Pahrump road."

"That's what I tried to..."

"Don't worry, this'll get us there."

The road was awful. Bouncy, dusty. Ernestine covered her mouth and nose with Kleenex because even with the windows closed, dust penetrated the motorhome. They were both coughing when Walter pulled into a gas station that looked like it could have been an old-time Western movie set. The RV's gas gauge was reading close to empty.

While a teenager with droopy pants filled the gas tank, Walter went in search of a phone book. Inside the station office, another kid sat in front of a full-on swamp cooler. His shirt was open and he was guzzling a Coke.

When Walter walked in, the kid jumped. "Oh geez, ya scared me. Can I help ya?"

"Do you have a phone book?"

The kid looked around, picked up some grimy papers from the top of the desk, and shrugged. "Guess not, what d'ya need?"

Walter explained about the motorhome and the air conditioning problem. "I need to find a repair shop."

"Well, there's a couple AC places in Vegas."

"That's where we're headed."

"But if it was my rig, I wouldn't take it to any of 'em. It'll cost ya big time."

"I expect it will, but I don't have much choice."

"Could I take a look?"

"You?"

"Yeah, I'm pretty good with that sorta thing."

Walter glared at the kid. "Well, I suppose you could look."

The kid's clothes and hands were black with grease, and Ernestine wasn't happy about him coming inside, especially after he removed the white louvered panel that covered the AC unit and left black fingerprints all over it. Her immediate urge was to grab a rag and a bottle of Mr. Clean. Instead, she stood aside while the kid told Walter what he thought the problem was.

"Looks like yer fan blade's rubbin' against the housing," the boy explained. "I can fix it for ya. Charge ya a lot less than them other guys."

Walter looked doubtful, and all Ernestine could think of was the grease the boy would leave on her pretty upholstery.

"Seriously, dude, I know this stuff. Watched my granddad do it for years."

"Is this your granddad's place then?" Ernestine asked. "This gas station?"

"Yeah, well, it is but—he's not here now. He's sick. Me and my brother Dale, we're runnin' the place."

The boys looked awfully young, sixteen and eighteen at most. "Sick how?" Ernestine asked. "Bad sick?" She hoped not. She hoped he'd be coming back.

"Not like cancer or anything. He's in a memory home. Old timers."

"Oh my. What about your folks? Do they help run this place?"

"Nope. They're not around. Granddad raised us."

What a shame, Ernestine thought, pushing away her dread of greasy fingers. These poor boys were trying to support themselves by keeping the business going. Giving them the work would be the right thing to do.

Walter must have been thinking the same thing, because when she looked at him, he nodded. "Okay," Ernestine said. "But what do we do while it's being worked on? Is there any place to stay around here?"

"There's a motel about a mile down the road. Pretty nice. My brother Dale can drive you there."

"Fine," Walter said. "We'd be much obliged."

Dale brought an old Nissan sedan, beat all to hell, from the back of the gas station and parked it by the Allegro. "Let me know when yer ready."

Seeing the car, Ernestine felt even worse for the boys. Not only did they have to run the business by themselves, but they didn't even have a decent car. She wondered how they were getting by and who took care of them. From the looks of them, nobody did. She imagined all sorts of difficulties the boys faced. She wanted to help and wondered if letting the older boy do the work on the air conditioner was enough. She knew those memory care places charged an arm and a leg and she hoped the granddad qualified for government help.

Even with her good intentions of helping the boys out, she was nervous about leaving the Allegro. It was, after all, stocked with food, some nice boxed wine, and lots of personal belongings. There was nothing she could do about that, though. They had to leave it unlocked so the kid could get inside to work on it.

She packed an overnight bag. A change of clothes for herself and Walter, toothbrushes and toothpaste, a deck of cards, and a can of disinfectant spray, just in case. In another bag, she put a box of crackers, a brick of cheese, bottles of water, a couple of cans of tuna, and a can opener. She left the motorhome and closed the door, then on second thought, went back and got one of the boxes of wine.

Walter climbed in the old Nissan beside the driver and Ernestine hunched in the musty, mushroomy-smelling back seat, hugging the overnight bags on her lap. The car creaked and jolted over potholes for about a mile before pulling into the Rattlesnake Inn, circa 1940, its flashing vacancy sign centered between two skinny palm trees. If the name wasn't disturbing enough, the appearance of the building was. There were eight units, all with faded red doors. The siding was covered with dust, weeds grew between the cracks of the broken walkway, and the whole thing sat so low to the ground it looked like a sunken ship.

"Are there any other motels?" she asked.

"Not till ya git closer to Vegas."

"We'll make it work," Walter said, handing the kid a ten-dollar bill. "Have your brother keep us posted on the air conditioner."

"Not real popular," Ernestine said looking around. There was only one car, an old Ford Pinto, parked in front of the place. Walking past it, she noticed the bright yellow license plate that screamed for attention. It seemed odd that, unlike most of the ones she'd seen, there was no slogan or anything, just the name of the state, OHIO, and the license number in red.

She knew she was being rude sniffing the air while she stood at the registration counter but she couldn't help it. She was sensitive to smells and squeamish about spending even one night in a place whose only other customer owned that beat-up Ford. She could hear a television playing somewhere in the back and after waiting for several minutes she cleared her throat.

Finally, a woman wearing an oversized plaid shirt and ripped jeans appeared looking annoyed at the interruption. Ernestine asked about the rate, and was quoted a price of ninety-seven dollars a night.

"My goodness that seems high," Ernestine said. "Do you have a senior citizen rate?"

"That is the senior rate," the woman snapped.

Thinking the price outrageous, and irked by the woman's attitude, Ernestine reluctantly handed over her credit card and began filling out the register. When she got to the line that asked for a license plate number, she said, "We're traveling in a motorhome. Our air conditioning went out. A kid dropped us off here."

The woman, showing no interest in Ernestine's circumstances, turned away without comment. Ernestine raised her voice. "It was unbearably hot without the AC so we left the rig with the young man at that gas station a mile back. Sad story there, the granddad being sick and all."

When the woman didn't respond, Ernestine went on, "I don't suppose many people stop here, do they?"

Still nothing.

"But I see you do have one other customer. From Ohio. I saw the license plate on that old car out there. Bright yellow with red letters. I don't remember seeing a plate like that before, with no slogan or anything."

The woman spun around and looked Ernestine in the eye. "Is there something else you need?"

"No, I was just trying to make conversation. I've never seen a license plate like that, have you?"

"Yes I have. That's my car. I'm from Ohio. It's bright yellow and plain because it designates a DUI driver. Is there anything else you want to know?"

Smarting like she'd been slapped, Ernestine went out to where Walter was waiting, handed him the room key, and said, "Well, she wasn't friendly."

The room was dark and smelled like the kid's Nissan, but the big, noisy swamp cooler was a blessing. Ernestine switched on the overhead light, checked for bugs in the bathroom, and turned down the bed to see if the sheets were clean. Then she unpacked her can of Lysol and sprayed the middle of the room, the curtains, the chair, the bathroom, and the carpet around the bed.

"What are you doing?" Walter asked, settling into a badly stained chair. "We're not going to catch anything."

Ernestine frowned. "What makes you think so? You don't know."

The next morning Ernestine woke with a crick in her back. The mattress had such a sag in the middle that she'd had to grip the edge of the bed all night to keep from plowing into Walter. At home, when her back hurt, she would get down on the floor and stretch, but the thought of even being barefoot on the filthy carpet made her cringe. She wasn't about to put her entire body on it. Groaning, she took her cosmetic case into the bathroom intending to take a shower. She pulled the curtain aside, and finding the rust-stained bathtub as discouraging as the carpet, she decided to forgo her usual morning routine.

Walter, on the other hand, sprang out of bed claiming he'd had the best night's sleep in a long while. "Did you say this place has a continental breakfast?"

The "Continental Breakfast" was a basket of cellophane-wrapped sweet rolls and some red delicious apples, only slightly bruised. There was a dispenser of orange juice, a hot-air pot that said COFFEE, a stack of paper cups, and nowhere to sit down. Walter filled a cup with the pale brown liquid and grabbed an apple. Ernestine did the same, and they retreated to their room.

Being in the literal middle of nowhere, they had nothing to do. Ernestine suggested they play gin-rummy, but after she dealt the cards Walter claimed he couldn't remember the rules. When she tried to explain them, he lost interest and turned on the TV. Then finding nothing but static and snow, he gave up and took a nap. At loose ends herself, Ernestine pulled the crossword book from her bag and worked on several of the unfinished puzzles.

The second day was more of the same. Ernestine felt listless. It was too hot to take a walk, there was nothing on TV, and she couldn't get Walter to play cards.

The third morning, Walter woke up stewing about getting on with the trip. "I'm going to walk back to that gas station and see how the kid's doing with the AC," he said. "I'm sure the other boy will give me a ride back."

Ernestine, tired of just sitting, was as ready as he was, but she didn't like the idea of him walking all that way in the heat. "Don't do it. It's too hot to be out there."

"I know it's hot."

"But you'll cook."

"No I won't. I'll be fine." Once he had on his shirt and trousers, he sat on the edge of the bed and bent over to put on his sandals. He fastened the strap on the left one, then stood and slid his right foot into the other.

"Ow, dammit! What was that?" He grabbed his foot and hopped to the chair.

"What is it? What happened?"

"Something bit me."

"What was it? Where?"

He pointed at the sandal just as a scorpion scurried out, tail in the air.

"Oh my God, oh my God! This is what I was afraid of." Frozen with fear, Ernestine watched the thing work its way across the carpet. When it got close to the door, she took off one of her shoes and threw it, missing the scorpion by a good two feet. She turned to look at Walter. He had started to wheeze, his head and neck were jerking, and his eyes were rolled back in his head. She needed to get help. But the scorpion was by the door. She would have to get past it to go out. She grabbed her iPhone and called 911.

11

When they got to the hospital, Walter's blood pressure was 197 over 92, high enough to cause alarm. Ernestine sat beside him the whole night praying. He spent the night sweating, vomiting, and groaning from pain. By morning his blood pressure was almost back to normal, but the young intern wanted to keep him another day for observation.

Now he lay on the hospital bed, his right foot sticking out from the sheet that covered the rest of him. A dark purplish rash embellished it from arch to ankle. Ernestine stayed until nightfall, watching him sleep fitfully, wake, and doze off again. When he appeared to be sleeping soundly, she left the room and called her daughter.

"Linda, it's Mom. We're in Las Vegas. Don't panic, but your dad's in the hospital."

"Oh my God! What happened?"

"He got stung by a scorpion at the motel."

There was a pause. "The motel? Why were you in a motel?"

"The motorhome's air conditioner stopped working. So we had to stay in a motel."

"I was afraid something like this would happen. You guys are too old to be out there on your own."

"Linda, it's only the air conditioner. It has nothing to do with how old we are."

"How long will they keep him?"

"Just one more day."

"Well then, when they discharge him, go home."

"No. We're not going home. This was your dad's dream trip. He's not going to let a little thing like this spoil it."

"So where are you now?"

"I'm still at the hospital."

"Are you okay? Do you need me to come?"

"No, I'm fine."

"Why haven't you called before now?"

"We were busy traveling. You could have called us."

"I tried, Mom, several times, but you didn't pick up. Do you have the ringer turned off?"

"I don't know. Where's the ringer."

"Oh God. Look on the left side, there's a little switch. I still think you should go home."

"No, I told you, we're not going to do that."

"Then will you at least call from time to time and let us know where you are? And have someone show you how to turn on the ringer."

When Ernestine hung up, her hands were shaking. Why did this always happen? Even when they agreed on things, Linda's bossiness provoked a stubborn response. She'd told Linda she was fine, but she wasn't. She had never been alone in a strange city. She needed to find a hotel room, but she couldn't think how to go about it. She would have to call a taxicab, but first she needed a phone book. And before she called a taxi, she needed to figure out where she was and where she wanted to go.

"Can I help you?" The nurse's rubber-soled shoes made no sound at all.

Ernestine jumped and clutched her heart. "Oh my goodness, you startled me."

"I'm sorry," the nurse said, "but do you need help with something? You've been standing here for quite some time and you look a bit lost."

Feeling foolish, Ernestine explained about the motor-home's air conditioner, the awful motel, the scorpion that had stung her husband, and that she didn't know how to go about finding a place to stay.

"May I?" The nurse held out her hand for Ernestine's phone. She tapped away on the little screen and within minutes had arranged for a cab and a hotel room, fixed the iPhone's ringer, and given Ernestine specific directions on where to meet her ride.

12

The next thing Ernestine knew, she was walking into the Trump Hotel. She crossed the lobby, all gold and white, its floors so mirror-like that the chandeliers seemed to be beneath her as well as above her. Behind the registration desk was an enormous brass etching that reminded her of Biblical characters. She gave the clerk her name and even though he didn't ask, explained why she didn't have any luggage, told him about Walter and the scorpion, and described the creepy motel. The clerk listened without comment, took her credit card, handed her a key-card, and pointed to a bank of elevators. "You're on the 35th floor."

She couldn't believe her eyes. The room was three times the size of the one at the Rattlesnake Inn and looked like a Martha Stewart magazine spread. Walls were a pale green, there was a gorgeous tapestry above the bed's padded headboard, and the bed with its fluffy white coverlet was piled with decorator pillows. Two elegant wing chairs faced a low, circular table topped with a flower arrangement, and in the corner, a bar with a small refrigerator and a cabinet filled with glassware.

Dumbfounded, she sat in one of the chairs and made another call to Linda. "You should see where I am," she said. "I'm at The Trump International Hotel. A nurse at the hospital made the reservation for me. It's amazing. And they only charged me a hundred and ten dollars. That can't be right, can it? I think they made a mistake. Do you think I should tell them?"

"Don't sweat it, Mom. They know what they're doing. They give you a discount price on the room and count on you losing a lot of money in the casino. So don't."

"Don't what?"

"Don't go to the casino. Those places take advantage of elderly people like you."

While she had Linda on the phone, Ernestine explored the rest of the room, describing it as she went. "Oh my, you should see this Jacuzzi tub and this picture window. The view is amazing. All those blinking, dancing, lights. I see signs for Jersey Boys. David Copperfield. Shania Twain. Cirque du Soliel. Oh, I wish you could see this."

"I've been to Vegas, Mom," Linda said. "You just stay in your room. Take a nice bath and get some rest. Call me tomorrow and let me know how Dad is."

Ernestine found the idea of a relaxing bath appealing, but she was hungry. She hadn't eaten anything since 7:00 a.m. when the nurse who came in to check Walter's vital signs noticed her and ordered a second breakfast brought to the room. Now it was nearly ten o'clock at night. At home, nothing would be open at this hour, but she could see tons of people milling around in the streets outside. Apparently time didn't matter in Las Vegas. She tucked her key-card into her pocketbook and headed for the elevator.

Going up thirty-five floors in the glass-walled elevator hadn't bothered her, but going down was different. The elevator dropped, sped up, stopped to pick up more passengers, and dropped again. Afraid she was going to be sick, she hung on to the handrail and closed her eyes. By the time they reached the lobby, she no longer felt like eating.

Hoping to settle her stomach, she stepped outside on shaky legs. It was still very warm, but the night air felt silky. She wished Walter was with her. She wondered if he would enjoy this or if he would be put off by the glitzy hotels and flashing lights. She was certain he'd have plenty to say about all the water fountains, especially considering the terrible drought they were having in California.

She walked a couple of blocks, taking in the sights, but her feet were starting to hurt. All the casinos were brightly lit and welcoming, so she went through a set of revolving doors and sat on a padded bench. It wasn't long before her curiosity got the better of her and she was drawn to where a couple dozen people were crushed against a table with a big red and black wheel.

Edging her way into the crowd, she asked a well-dressed old gentleman, "What is this?"

"Roulette, my dear," he said. "Have you never played?"

"No."

"Would you like to know how it works?"

She nodded.

After a complicated explanation that left her confused, she felt obligated to put five dollars on the table, if for no other reason than to repay the gentleman for his tutelage.

As he instructed, she placed one-dollar chips on five different numbers. The wheel spun, and when one of her numbers came up she was given thirty-five chips. She was astonished.

"Go again," the man encouraged.

Covering five more numbers, she scored a second time. She looked back at the man and when he nodded, she went again. Her chips started to pile up and people were starting to watch her. It would be crazy to quit now. A girl came by with a tray of cocktails and she took one.

"Try ten dollars next time," the old fellow said.

She stacked ten chips and placed them all on number 23, Walter's birthday, and held her breath as she waited for the wheel to stop. When it stopped on 23, she squealed with delight and pulled more chips into her growing mound.

"You're on a roll, madam," the old man said. "Why don't you try playing corners or halves?"

"What do you mean?"

Reaching over her shoulder, he picked up one of her chips and placed it where four numbers intersected. "If any of these four numbers come up, you win eight dollars to every one dollar you bet. That's called playing corners. If you put your chips on the line between two numbers and one of them comes up, it's called playing halves. That pays seventeen to one."

"What the heck," she said, putting her entire winnings on the line straddling 22/23. The wheel spun and landed on ...16.

A collective groan rose from the people around the table. Disappointed, Ernestine turned to say something to her adviser, but he was nowhere to be seen.

She knew she'd really only lost her initial five dollars and that all the rest was "house money," but while she was raking in the winnings, it was hers. Now that it was gone, she felt empty, expectant, like she needed something to fill the void. The cocktail waitress came by and Ernestine accepted another drink. Sipping it, she ambled toward the slot machines. Suddenly, she was grabbed by a woman whose machine was discharging earsplitting bells and flashing lights. "I won! I won!" the woman screamed, jostling Ernestine as she jumped up and down. "I just won five hundred dollars!"

Caught up in the woman's excitement, Ernestine slid onto the seat of the adjacent machine, put a five dollar bill into the slot, and when the waitress came by a third time, she exchanged her empty glass for a full one.

13

Ernestine woke up fully clothed on top of the pretty white duvet. She had a killer headache, a churning stomach, and a vague feeling that she'd lost a lot of money. She remembered watching red 7s and cherries spin and stop. She remembered bells and lights. And she remembered pushing the spin button over and over and over. What she didn't remember was how she got back to her room. With a pounding heart, she checked her pocketbook for money and found only a twenty and a couple of ones. She tried to remember how much she had started with. Even more disturbing was the fact that, instead of being in the zippered section where she kept it secure, her credit card was loose on the bottom of the bag. The last time she remembered using it was when she'd paid for the room. Had she forgotten to put it back? She didn't know.

She looked at the pretty Jacuzzi tub but opted instead for a quick shower. After putting on the clothes she had just taken off, she left the room, but not before rehanging the bath towels and smoothing the bedding.

Now that she knew what taxi company to call, she could arrange for transportation back to the hospital, and once Walter was discharged, get them a ride to where they had left the Allegro. But first she needed to get something to eat.

After several cups of coffee and a few nibbles of a ham and cheese omelet, her hands stopped shaking and she felt strong enough to face the hospital ... and Walter.

He was dressed and sitting in a chair. "Where did you go?"

"I couldn't sleep here, so I went to a hotel. How do you feel? Are they discharging you?"

"They say I can leave as soon as they do the paperwork." He held up his foot for her to see. It was still a bit swollen, but the redness and rash were gone.

With the discharge papers in her hand, Ernestine called a taxi to take them back to the gas station. She wasn't thrilled about taking a taxi again, especially since the ride from the hospital to the Trump Hotel last night had cost over fifty-two dollars and she'd paid the same to come back here this morning. She didn't want to tell Walter what it cost. She didn't want to talk about money at all.

Walter tried to make conversation with the cabbie, but once he realized the man didn't speak English, he gave up and the car grew silent. Ernestine was reluctant to say anything about her stay at the hotel for fear that Walter would ask about the cost, and she would end up having to tell him about the casino. After fifteen minutes, however, the silence was too much for her to bear.

"Is there something wrong, Walter?" she asked. "You're so quiet."

"I miss my cat."

"Your cat? You haven't mentioned her since we left Yosemite. I didn't know it was still bothering you."

"Why wouldn't it? I loved that cat. I've just had... all this other stuff to worry about."

"Do you want to go back to Yosemite and see if we can find her?"

"No. I miss her but I don't want to go back."

Ernestine patted Walter's hand, all the while keeping an eye on the taxi's meter. She could feel her blood pressure rise with every click. By the time they got to the service station, it had reached $98.40. With trembling fingers, she slid the credit card through the reader and okayed a fifteen percent tip.

"Got'er fixed," the boy said, handing Walter a bill. "Come to more than I thought, though. Turned out it weren't just yer fan blade. Replaced the compressor too."

Without saying a word, Walter glanced at the bill and passed it to Ernestine. It was almost five hundred dollars, twice what she had guessed it would be. With a sick feeling, she handed the boy the credit card and signed her name on the receipt.

"Oh, forgot to tell ya. We left the generator runnin' overnight to make sure the AC worked. Used up all yer propane."

"Oh, don't worry about that," Walter said, "Need to refill the tank soon anyway."

"Nice and cool in here now," Walter said as he drove back to the Rattlesnake Inn to settle the bill. "It's a good thing I took that dirt road when I did. A regular repair shop would have charged a lot more."

"Yeah, it's a good thing," Ernestine shot back. "You wouldn't have gotten the scorpion bite or got to stay in that nice hospital either."

As soon as that was out of her mouth, she wished she hadn't said it. There was no point in taking her worries out on Walter. She could almost hear the *ca-ching, ca-ching, ca-ching* as she mentally added the four hundred ninety-six dollar repair bill to the taxi rides, the three days at the motel, two of which they weren't even there, and the room at the Trump Hotel. Not to mention what she might have lost at the casino.

After paying the bill at the motel and retrieving the items they'd left there, they headed for the interstate.

"Do you mind if we skip Las Vegas?" Walter said. "I don't need to see that place."

With a sense of relief, Ernestine opened the Good Sam book to the map of Nevada. "Well, it looks like we can avoid it by going to Henderson, and from there we can head to Kingman, Arizona. You said you wanted to see Route 66."

"That sounds good," Walter said. "When we get to Henderson, let's stop and you can fix us some lunch."

While Walter drove, Ernestine picked up a paperback and tried to read, but she couldn't concentrate. All the letters looked like dollar signs. The credit card was the first one she'd ever had, and the bank had allowed her a five thousand dollar credit limit. Initially, that sounded like more than enough. But with the way things were adding up, and not knowing how much she might have put on the card at the casino, the fear of exceeding that limit had her shaking in her Nikes.

Walter parked the rig in a city park in Henderson and Ernestine went back to the kitchen to fix some lunch. When she opened the little refrigerator the smell nearly knocked her over. Holding her nose, she slid open the vegetable drawer. Lettuce, green onions, broccoli, limp and wilted, swam in a half-inch of green goo. She opened the freezer compartment. The chicken tenders and pre-marinated steaks were thawed and sweating. She squeezed the container of Ben & Jerry's ice cream and watched it ooze from around the lid. "Oh my God," she wailed. "Everything is ruined."

Just like running into the wall at Linda's, and having the bear tear out the window at Yosemite, things Ernestine found catastrophic didn't faze Walter. While she carried on about the mess and the expense, cleaned the refrigerator and threw all the spoiled food away, he acted as though nothing had happened. "I thought we were going to have some lunch."

"Didn't you just watch me throw all the food out?"

"But I'm hungry."

"Oh, for crying out loud." Ernestine took a loaf of bread and a jar of peanut butter out of the cupboard and made him a sandwich.

"Didn't that kid tell you he'd used up all our propane?"

"Did he? I don't remember."

"He did. Could that be why the refrigerator doesn't work?"

"The refrigerator doesn't work?"

"Damn it, Walter. What's the matter with you?" Ernestine couldn't believe her ears. Could he really not remember about the propane tank? Could he really not understand that the refrigerator didn't work? Biting her tongue so as not to yell at him, she got the Good Sam book and looked for a place where they could refill the propane tank and get a few groceries.

"There's an RV Park in Boulder City that advertises an on-sight store with all manner of camping gear," she said, but we'll need to backtrack a few miles."

Once they were turned around, she felt bad about snapping at him. His not remembering the empty propane tank was troubling, but it wasn't his fault the food spoiled. And it wasn't really him she was mad at anyway. It was her bad judgment that was eating at her. She was the one who might have lost a lot of money in a casino. It was just easier to be mad at Walter.

14

After they replenished the propane and picked up a few over-priced grocery items at the RV Park store, Ernestine, itching to walk off her irritation, suggested they take a stroll and get a look at Lake Mead. She stomped on ahead of Walter, slowing every now and then to let him catch up, and then out-pacing him again. They'd gone about a mile when he called from behind her, "Stop. My foot hurts. I want to go back." She turned around. He was sitting on a big rock with his right pant leg rolled up and he'd taken off his shoe. His ankle was swollen to twice its normal size, and an ugly red rash ran from the top of his foot to his knee. Ernestine's first thought was that the poison from the scorpion sting had come back. Her second thought was that she shouldn't have suggested a walk in the first place.

Leaving him there, she raced back to the campground and burst into the office. "Can someone go pick up my husband? He's about a mile up the road and his foot is all red and swollen." She had to stop to catch her breath. "And he can't walk."

Roberta, the manager, tsk-tsked in sympathy and called for her husband to help.

At a nearby Urgent Care clinic, the doctor didn't agree with Ernestine's diagnosis. "This wouldn't be caused by a scorpion sting," he said. "Mr. Emmons, are you a golfer?"

"Never played golf in my life."

"Well, in this heat this can happen. I see it all the time. It's called golfer's vasculitis."

Walter tried to contradict him, but the doctor was busily writing on a note pad. "Here," he said tearing a sheet off the pad, "get a tube of this cortisone cream and refrain from playing golf for at least a week."

Annoyed by the doctor's manner, Walter spent the rest of the evening complaining that his foot was killing him and ignoring Ernestine's suggestion that he keep it elevated. After several hours of frustration, she left him sitting up and went to bed.

She was almost asleep when the whole rig started to rumble and shake. "What the—" She got up and stormed to the front of the rig where Walter was standing beside the control panel. "Walter!" she yelled. "Stop!"

"What? What's the matter?"

"You're closing the slide out! You can't do that now. What in heaven's name are you thinking?"

"Aren't we leaving?"

"No, we're not leaving. It's the middle of the night. Get away from that thing."

Looking hurt, he headed for the bedroom, mumbling that they needed to get going. Now it was Ernestine's turn to stay up and stew. What in the world was going on with him? Just now he'd tried to close the slide out, earlier he'd forgotten about the empty propane tank, and he hadn't gotten the connection between her throwing out all the food and not fixing lunch. Could all this have to do with that scorpion sting, she wondered. Could it have affected his brain?

By morning, his rash was gone, but his foot was still so swollen he couldn't get his right shoe on. He was, however, able to drive wearing his bedroom slippers, and after an hour or so on the road Ernestine spotted a Walmart and insisted they stop.

"I just need a few things," she said. "I'll try to hurry. You stay here. You can't go in without shoes."

"Sure I can. I'll wear my slippers. Nobody will notice." With Walter trailing behind her, Ernestine rushed through the grocery department and the checkout line, and as they were leaving the store, they passed a mom and two little girls, with a box of kittens. Ernestine hurried past with no more than a glance. The motorhome was parked at the far end of the lot, and she didn't want to take a chance on spoiling any of the food she'd just purchased.

"I paid way too much for those Stouffer's frozen dinners you like so much," she said, thinking Walter was right behind her. "I can't believe how high the prices are here. Did you see how much they wanted for bacon? I'm not paying that. You'll just have to go without..."

Bacon was just about Walter's favorite thing, and when he didn't protest, she turned around and saw that he wasn't even with her. He was back by the store's exit, bent over the box of kittens.

Annoyed, she pushed the cart all the way back. "For God's sake, Walter, come on. I need to get this food in the refrigerator or we'll lose it too."

Walter picked up one of the kittens and nuzzled it. "Just give me a minute. Look at this one. Her black and orange markings are like Vivian's." He held it up and looked at her little face. "I think we should take her."

"You're not serious. A kitten in a motorhome?"

"Yes, I'm serious. I miss my cat. This little thing won't be any trouble."

The older girl, who looked about six, watched Walter expectantly.

"How much?" he asked.

"They're free," the girl sniffed. "Our daddy won't let us keep them. We have three cats and a puppy and he says it's enough already."

Walter pulled out his wallet and handed the little girl a ten-dollar bill. "You take this anyway."

He let the teary-eyed girls give the kitten a goodbye pet, and then he curled it into his chest and headed for the motorhome. Ernestine, following him this time, wheeled the shopping cart back across the hot asphalt.

While she got busy in the kitchen, Walter sat on the sofa and petted the kitten. It began to purr, and Walter's breathing slowed. Halfway through putting the groceries away, she looked over and saw they were both asleep. In spite of her misgivings, the scene made her smile. When she finished putting things in place, she took the cart and went back to the store for a bag of cat food and a new supply of kitty litter.

They named her Yosie, short for Yosemite, where Vivian had taken a powder. And, like Ernestine had predicted, the feisty kitten became a menace. She would sit between the two front seats and watch Walter drive, then, without warning, lunge at him and attach herself to the right sleeve of his shirt with her sharp little claws. Other times, she'd climb to the top of his head and bat at his glasses. Once, when he removed her, she pounced on his still-sore right foot, causing him to swerve dangerously. Ernestine attempted to keep the kitten confined by placing her in the bathroom while they were traveling, but every now and then when they hit a bump, the bathroom door flew open and Yosie made a dive for Walter.

In spite of the kitten's treacherous antics, Ernestine grew fond of her. She got a kick out of watching the tiny bundle of energy skitter around chasing a piece of string or tangling herself in the ball of yarn they bought for her. Ernestine even excused her for sharpening her claws on the upholstery. Walter, on the other hand, said it had been a mistake. "I wish we'd gotten a puppy instead."

15

Leaving Boulder City, Walter started recounting the history of Hoover Dam. He'd seen a documentary about its construction during the Great Depression, and he couldn't wait to drive over it and see it for himself.

"It's not open to through traffic," Ernestine said, referencing the Good Sam guide in her lap.

"Oh sure it is. Richard and Shirley..."

"No it's not, Walter. It says right here: 'THE DAM IS NOT OPEN TO THROUGH TRAFFIC.' We can drive across and park. See the visitor center. But you'll have to turn the rig around in the parking lot and come all the way back."

"Well, that's not a problem."

"Yes, it is a problem. The visitor center is a long walk from the parking lot. With your swollen foot..."

"Let me worry about my foot."

"Okay, but listen to this: 'ALL RECREATIONAL TYPE VEHICLES WILL BE SUBJECT TO AN INSPECTION BY A BUREAU OF RECLAMATION POLICE OFFICER.'"

"Inspection for what?"

"I don't know. Drugs, I suppose, or explosives.

"We don't need to be searched."

"I know. I know."

"Well then," Walter said, "if they're going to do that, let's skip the damn dam." With that settled, he headed toward the Mike O'Callaghan-Pat Tillman Memorial Bridge downstream.

At the bridge, Ernestine, having read that it was nine hundred feet in the air over the Colorado River, squeezed her eyes shut and began making a low moaning noise.

"What's with you?" Walter asked.

"I can't look."

"There's nothing to see. The walls are so high you couldn't see the river if you tried."

She kept her eyes closed anyway, and concentrated on the whump-whump noise for the entire nineteen hundred feet across the bridge.

"You can open your eyes now," Walter said when he hit the pavement on the other side. "We're in Arizona."

Fort Beale RV Park in Kingman offered "LONG/WIDE PULL-THRUS" and a swimming pool. "A swim would feel good right now," Ernestine said. "I think I'm going to like this place."

Once they got settled, Walter agreed the water might make his foot feel better. He couldn't remember the last time he'd been in a swimming pool, or in a pair of swim trunks for that matter. While he was getting changed, Ernestine came out of the little bathroom holding her new two-piece suit in one hand and a drenched and dripping kitten in the other. Yosie looked more like a drowned rat than a kitten.

"Dammit Walter! You forgot to close the toilet lid again. I don't know how many times I have to tell you. How would you feel if she fell in there and drowned?" Yosie squirmed out of Ernestine's grasp and scurried under the dinette table. Down on her knees, Ernestine pulled the kitten out, wrapped her in a towel, and rubbed her fur until she was almost dry. By now, she was out of the mood to go swimming, but Walter was standing outside the motorhome calling for her to hurry up. She wiggled into her swimming suit and, seeing herself in the mirrored closet door, wrapped an enormous beach towel around her waist and joined him.

The pool was crowded with screaming children and several adults who seemed to be paying no attention to them. Walter and Ernestine eased into the shallow end of the pool, gasping from the cold with each forward step. They were about neck deep when a young boy cannon-balled into the pool, bombarding them with a tidal wave of water. Sputtering and trying to shake the water off his glasses, Walter yelled, "You little shit, come back here."

The boy, already out of the pool and preparing to jump in front of another couple, turned in Walter's direction and lifted his middle finger.

"You yellin' at my kid?" A man with an enormous beer belly stood glowering down at Walter.

"You're damn right I am. He cannon-balled right in front of us and he didn't even apologize."

"Hell, it's a pool. You're supposed to get wet."

"I want him to apologize."

"I want him to apologize," the man mimicked in a falsetto voice.

Ernestine could tell that, even in the cold water, Walter's blood was starting to boil.

"Come on," she said taking his arm, "Let's go."

"Not until I have an apology."

"Come *on*," she urged, tugging harder. He wouldn't budge. The longer he stood there, the redder his face got, and then suddenly he grabbed his chest.

"Oh my God," Ernestine said, "he's having a heart attack. Someone call 911."

Hearing this, the kid's dad jumped into the pool, hauled Walter out of the water, and started doing chest compressions. By the time the ambulance arrived, people had gathered to gawk.

The EMTs took over, checking Walter's vital signs and fitting him with an oxygen mask. "We need to take him to the hospital," one of the EMTs told Ernestine. "It could be a heart attack or it could be something else. But we need to be sure."

Walter shook his head and tried to sit say something but with the oxygen mask on it was unintelligible.

The paramedic looked at Ernestine.

"He said he doesn't want to go to the hospital again. He just got out."

"Oh, why was that?"

"He got stung by a scorpion and it made him real sick."

"Sir," the EMT said, "we're taking you in. You can't afford to ignore this."

Everybody had gotten out of the pool and stood watching while Walter was lifted into the back of the ambulance. If that child had had a decent upbringing, she thought as she climbed in behind the gurney, this wouldn't have happened.

16

You can button your shirt now," the ER doctor said after he'd given Walter a thorough examination. "Have you ever had an angina attack before?"

Walter shook his head. "What's angina?"

"It happens when your heart muscle isn't getting enough oxygen-rich blood. It's a warning sign of heart disease. Stress can bring it on."

"I don't have any stress," Walter said. "I'm retired."

"Well apparently you had some today."

"What? Oh, well, that little shit..."

The doctor raised his eyebrows?

"It was a kid in the swimming pool," Ernestine said. "Got him all upset."

The doctor cleared his throat. "Mr. Emmons. You didn't have a heart attack this time. But there could be one in your future if you don't take care of yourself. Avoid stress. Watch your diet. Cut down on red meat." He turned to leave and with his hand on the doorknob, said, "Mrs. Emmons, I'm sending him out of here with some nitroglycerin tablets. They're to be used in an emergency. Instructions will be on the bottle."

Walter having a heart attack was Ernestine's worst nightmare, and the doctor's brusque manner left her feeling irritable and vindicated at the same time. She was aware that Walter's diet wasn't ideal, and now she felt guilty for allowing him to eat whatever he wanted. And as for stress, wasn't this trip supposed to be relaxing?

She knew she should call Linda and tell her what had happened, but she couldn't face another lecture about their age, their inexperience, and their vulnerability.

That night she didn't sleep well. She couldn't stop thinking about how worked up Walter got over having water splashed on him, and she wondered how he'd react when he found out she'd lost money in Las Vegas. It might be enough to kill him.

When Walter awoke the next morning ready to hit the road, she appealed for additional time. "Let's stay here for a while," she said handing him his coffee. "This is a nice park, and that doctor said you should rest and avoid stress."

"He said nothing of the sort."

"He did. That's what he said."

"Bullshit."

Ernestine turned back to the electric griddle and cracked an egg next to the two pancakes. "Yes he did. He said avoid stress. Those were his exact words."

"I don't care what he said. I don't want to stay here. I don't like these people."

"What people?"

"That big guy and his smart-ass kid, that's what people. We're not staying here."

She slid the pancakes and egg onto a plate and set it in front of him. "Driving is stressful and you shouldn't be doing it right now."

"Then you drive."

"I can't. I don't know how to drive this thing."

"Well then, I'm driving."

She was losing the argument, and given Walter's angina attack, she didn't want a full-blown battle. She was going to have to let him drive.

While he undid the connections and stowed things away, she washed the dishes and fed the kitten. When he came back inside, she continued to putter around, straightening up and dusting.

"Come on," he said, "you can do that later. Put your clothes on. We need to get going."

She took her time getting dressed and arranging the furniture so the slide outs could be closed, then giving in to his impatience, she settled into the passenger seat. Walter started the engine, released the emergency brake, crept out of the campsite onto 4th Street, and turned left on Andy Devine Avenue.

"Now this here," he said, "is Historic Route 66. Keep your eyes open, there's a lot to see."

Before they had gone far, a car pulled out and passed the motorhome at what Ernestine thought an ungodly speed. "Did you see that license plate, Walter? I'll bet it's one of those drunk drivers."

"What are you talking about?"

"It was one of those bright yellow ones with red letters like we saw at the motel. The DUI one."

"Come on. The one on that car was New Mexico."

"Well, help me watch, will you? I don't want to be anywhere near a drunk driver."

"You know, Ernie, those plates don't mean the driver's drunk, it only means they've been ticketed for that before."

"Well, if they did it once..."

"Oh, for Pete's sake, you're being silly."

She dropped the subject. It was just another example of how he didn't take serious things seriously. She tried to relax and watch for "historical" things, but all she saw were abandoned buildings, pieces of rusted machinery, and broken-down cars. "What is it I'm supposed to be seeing on Route 66? It looks pretty deserted to me."

"That's the history. In the '50s when the interstate came through most of the businesses closed up. There's supposed to be a general store up here a ways that's still open. I'm going to pull in when we get there. I want to look around."

Unimpressed, Ernestine kept watching. Besides the litter and rusted cars, there were frequent billboards. She read each one aloud: HISTORIC ROUTE 66, SEE AMERICA'S

WONDERLAND, ROUTE 66 RESTAURANT, BEST BURGERS. They passed one that said ROADKILL CAFE 60 MILES AHEAD. She was about to comment on the name, when a huge buck leapt in front of them and hit the left front of the motorhome. Walter swerved, stomped on the brake, hit loose gravel, and slid the distance of a football field. They came to a stop crosswise on the pavement with their front end facing the center line.

For Ernestine, those five or six seconds felt like forever. The image of that poor, defenseless animal was burned into her brain and she began to shake.

"It's okay, Ernie," Walter said, gripping her forearm. "We're okay. We're fine. Nobody got hurt?"

"The deer did. The deer got hurt. "

"Look, I know, but there's nothing we can do about it. People hit deer all the time."

She undid her seatbelt. "The poor thing. I need to go see."

Walter kept hold of her arm. "You can't go back there. If it is alive, it's hurt, and it'll be dangerous. Sit down. I need to get off the highway." He let go of her arm and eased the motorhome off the pavement.

Still shaking, Ernestine moved to the swivel rocker behind the cab and Walter stepped down onto the roadside. Almost immediately, an orange and black Highway Patrol vehicle pulled up behind the motorhome.

The officer towered over Walter. "You all right?"

"I'm fine," Walter said looking up at him.

"Anyone with you?"

"The wife's inside."

The officer stuck his head in the open door. "Ma'am? Are you okay?"

Startled by her double image in the officer's mirrored aviator glasses, Ernestine jumped. "Uh yes, I'm okay, but I think we killed that poor deer."

"Yes, ma'am, you did."

Returning to his vehicle, the officer took some neon orange cones from the back and set them behind the motorhome. Once he had the traffic diverted, he got a notebook from his car and came back to where Walter stood, still in his bedroom slippers, staring at the damage. The whole front left section of the RV was caved in and the headlight assembly looked like an eyeball hanging from its socket.

"Damn shame," the officer said. "How fast were you going?"

"The speed limit I guess."

The officer nodded and mopped his forehead. "Hotter'n blazes out here. Mind if we go inside? I'll need to see your driver's license and we'll have to fill out an accident report."

Intimidated by the man's size, and his gun, Ernestine stood aside to let him come in. He squeezed into the bench behind the dinette, bumped his gun on the table's edge, and sat on the tail of the kitten who bared her claws and scratched his arm as she darted free.

"Come here, sweetheart," Ernestine said picking up the kitten and petting her before putting her in the lavatory and closing the door.

Dabbing at the blood on his arm with his handkerchief, the patrolman went through the three-page report question by question. Driver and ownership information, make, model, VIN number, insurance policy information, whether anyone was injured, an estimate of an injury severity, the posted speed limit, light condition, weather condition, manner of crash impact, road surface condition, direction of travel, contributing circumstances, road grade, and there was a section for a diagram and accident description written like a story from the officer's point of view.

By the time they were finished, Walter was sweating bullets. If hitting the deer wasn't stressful enough, Ernestine thought, this accident report might cause him to have a real heart attack.

"Hang onto that," the officer said handing Walter a copy of the report. "Where you folks headed?"

"Grand Canyon."

"That's quite a ways yet. You sure you want to continue? I can call you a tow truck."

"No," Walter said. "We've come this far. I think we're fine."

"Well alright, but you'll need to get that headlight fixed asap. You can't be driving at night with one headlight."

The RV's shock-absorbers gave an audible groan as the officer stepped out. "I'll follow you for a stretch," he said, "make sure you're all right. And we'll take care of the animal." He winked at Walter. "Maybe take it up to that Roadkill Café."

Walter climbed up front, put on his seatbelt, and pulled forward onto the asphalt. The motorhome ran smoothly, and after a short distance the patrolman dropped back. As she watched Walter drive, Ernestine reflected on the trip so far. Hitting the deer was just the latest disaster in a trip that was becoming a nightmare. The financial hole they were digging kept getting deeper, and she still hadn't told Walter about Las Vegas. Just as that thought crossed her mind, she realized that he hadn't even been mentioning the cost of things. And that was strange. His penchant for pinching pennies was well known, but since the thing in Las Vegas, she'd been so focused on what she might have done that she hadn't noticed his lack of concern.

"Walter," she said, "let's go home. I think hitting that deer was an omen. I think it means we shouldn't be doing this."

He didn't answer and she didn't push, she just leaned forward, practically smooshing her nose against the glass, and watched for deer.

17

Ernestine was still upset about hitting the deer when they got to Hackberry and the General Store that Walter wanted to see. In her opinion, the place was an eyesore. Every square inch of the corrugated aluminum building was covered with junk. There was a Mobil Pegasus Flying Red Horse sign, Coca Cola coolers, several old gas pumps, rusted out trucks, classic cars, and old engines. And tourists were crawling all over the place.

"See what I told you," Walter said, pulling into the parking lot. "This place is great. Let's take a look around." He climbed out the door and Ernestine followed. She hadn't yet seen the damage from hitting the deer, so she walked around to the front.

"Oh my God, this is terrible."

"Ah, it's fine. A little duct tape will fix it right up."

Irritated, and not really interested in seeing the store, she climbed back inside and sat at the table. The officer had warned them not to drive at night without a headlight so they needed to find a place to camp before it got dark, and this stop at the general store was wasting time they didn't have.

She heard a buzzing noise, but didn't know where it was coming from. Then she heard it again and realized it was the cell phone. It was Linda, the last person on earth she wanted to talk to right now. She took a deep breath, slid her finger across the little bar and answered.

"Oh, Linda, is that you?"

"Yes, Mom. Who else would it be? Why didn't you answer the first time?"

"It took me a minute to find the phone."

"Where are you guys? I've been worried."

"We're in Arizona. On Route 66. At a general store. Your dad is having a great time looking at all this old stuff."

"Why haven't you called? Is everything all right?"

"Everything's fine. Well—" Ernestine started to tell her about hitting the deer but thought better of it. Linda was so condescending, so bossy, if she knew about this, she'd start nagging her again about going home.

"What, Mom?"

"Oh, nothing—"

"You got the AC fixed, didn't you?"

"Yes, it's fixed."

"Mom, you started to say something. What was it?"

Ernestine searched her head for something. "Uh, I was going to tell you we got a new kitten."

"Mom? A kitten? Did something happen to Vivian?"

"She ran away. At Yosemite. Jumped out and ran off. We looked, but never found her. Your dad missed her, so we got a kitten. Sweet little thing. Yosie. For Yosemite."

"Jesus, Mom. That's just what you guys need. It'll be trouble."

"She's no trouble. Don't worry." Anxious to end the conversation, Ernestine said, "I gotta go. Your dad's calling me. Be sure to tell Matt and the boys I said hello."

"Mom ... Mom? Call more often will you?"

"Yes, dear, I will."

Feeling like she'd dodged a bullet, Ernestine climbed out of the motorhome and joined Walter, who seemed riveted by all the memorabilia. She left him and wandered inside the store. She couldn't believe how cluttered the place was. Old license plates covered the ceiling, hubcaps and rusted metal signs advertising products that in some cases hadn't existed for decades, lined the walls. It was jam-packed with 1950's era souvenirs, everything from keychains and magnets to full-size jukeboxes. She didn't see anything she wanted, and certainly nothing she needed. Spotting a rack of baseball caps, she picked out a white one with a Route 66 patch on the front.

"Now that suits you," Walter said when she came out of the store wearing it. "And it'll keep the sun out of your eyes."

She didn't think it suited her at all. She'd only bought it because she was being eyeballed by the cashier who seemed to suspect she might shoplift something.

"Speaking of the sun," she said, tugging on his arm, "we need to get going. It'll be dark before we know it and we can't drive at night without a headlight, remember?"

"Just a few more minutes. I want to get another look at that '56 Corvette. I always wanted one of those. Couldn't afford one once we had Linda and you stopped working."

Surprised, she wondered where that came from. He'd never grumbled about her not working before. In fact it had always been his idea.

She started to follow him to where the Corvette was, but then she noticed a barefoot and filthy young girl sitting on a bench beside a wooden Indian. The girl wore ragged jeans and a T-shirt that stretched tight across a pregnant belly.

When Ernestine approached, the girl lifted a cardboard sign that read: NEED A LIFT, GOING EAST.

Catching up with Walter, Ernestine pointed in the girl's direction and pleaded with her eyes.

"No," he said. "Not a chance."

"But look at her."

"No."

"I'm going to go talk to her."

Walking back to the girl Ernestine said, "What's your name, honey?"

"Clover."

"I'm Ernestine. How old are you, Clover?"

"Seventeen."

"Are you here alone?"

"Uh-huh. My boyfriend and me, we had a fight."

"A fight?"

"Yeah," she wiped her nose on her sleeve and put one hand on her belly. "He was, like, taking me to see my mom. But he, like, changed his mind."

"He didn't just leave you here, did he?"

"Uh huh. He said he doesn't want the baby. Said he wasn't ready." She stopped and looked down. "I wasn't ready either but I don't, like, have a choice."

"And where is your mom?"

"Manhattan."

"Oh my," Ernestine said. "We're not planning to go that far."

"But if you could, like, just get me somewhere east of here. Colorado even, maybe then I can find another ride."

"I don't know," Ernestine said. "My husband, he doesn't like the idea of picking up hitchhikers. But come with me. We'll ask him."

"Just a minute. I have to go get my things." The girl got up and disappeared around the back of the building. When she returned, she had a big backpack and a chocolate lab puppy.

Walter had already said no, but then he saw the dog.

18

While Walter drove, Ernestine sat with the girl at the dinette table. She reached down to stroke the puppy. "What's his name?"

"Chocolate Chip. I call him Chip."

"That's cute. He's housebroken isn't he?"

"Oh, yeah. He's good. Still squats to pee though. I guess they, like, learn to lift their leg later."

Ernestine smiled and patted the puppy again. Just then Yosie, the kitten, crawled off the bed in the back and stretched her way forward. The puppy woofed and lunged, getting a quick lesson in the form of claws across his nose. Chip whimpered and curled himself under Clover's feet, while the kitten, looking satisfied, sat and began cleaning herself.

"I guess he won't do that again," Ernestine said with a chuckle.

Clover stroked the puppy. "He's never been around cats before."

For a moment Ernestine just sat and watched the girl. She wondered if she was doing the right thing in letting her come along. She'd heard stories about people being ripped off, even killed, by hitchhikers. But this girl, Clover she called herself, seemed so gentle, so genuine, and so vulnerable.

"Clover," she said, "tell me about yourself. Where are you from?"

"Kansas. Well, like, that's where I was born. But I've been in California."

"Didn't you say your mother lives in Manhattan?"

"She does. But I grew up with my dad in Moline. My mom didn't live with us."

"Oh. And how was it you happened to be in California?"

"Well, me and my friend Jenna went out there to look for jobs. Like, you know, in the movies or, like, modeling."

"And you thought that'd be easy to do?"

"Well, yeah. People were always saying how pretty we were and ... but it's not easy at all. I found that out."

"Had you finished school?"

"No. We quit."

"What did your folks think about that?"

"We didn't tell them. Not till, like, later."

Ernestine took in the girl's greasy hair, chipped fingernails, and dirty feet. "California's a long way from Kansas. How did you get there?"

"Hitched."

"Hitchhiked? Oh my goodness. That's so dangerous."

107

"It was fine. Truckers like having somebody to talk to. We'd ride with one guy for a while, then, when he, like, got where he was going, we'd hook up with somebody else."

"Were you scared? I would have been."

"Not at first. Most of 'em were real nice. Bought us food and sodas. But then Jenna got homesick. Didn't want to go any more. She got a ride with a guy who was going back to Kansas." Clover picked at a fingernail that was chewed down to the quick and bore traces of weeks-old nail polish.

"Was it scarier alone?"

"Yeah. A lot. I got a lift from this one dude who turned out to be a real pig. Put his hands all over me. Said if I wouldn't let him, you know, he'd drop me off in the middle of nowhere."

"And?"

"And I wouldn't. So he kicked me out."

"Oh, honey, that's terrible. What did you do?"

"Well, I walked for a long ways. I wasn't sure about taking another ride after what happened, but I was, like, tired of walking."

"And the next person was okay?"

"Uh-huh, it was a lady. In, like, an awesome Beamer. She took me all the way to Lodi where she lived. Even let me stay at her house."

"That was nice, right?"

"It was okay for a little while. I got a job at a place bussing tables, but it sucked. The pay was lousy and the manager was always hitting on me. Then I met this guy. Said with my looks, he could get me a job in L.A."

Clover flipped her long stringy hair over one shoulder and toyed with the split ends.

"And did he?"

"What, get me a job? Shit, no. We got to Culver City and he told me to get out of the car. Said he'd be in touch. I, like, never heard from him again."

"What did you do then?"

"Slept a couple nights in the bus station and met some other people who, like me, were looking for work in the" — she made air-quotes — "industry."

"The movies?"

"Yeah, or modeling."

Ernestine let her eyes linger on Clover's belly. "Is that where you met this boyfriend?"

"Marcus? Uh-huh. He's really talented but, like, he can't even get an audition."

"You moved in together?"

"Yeah. Well, we all did. Three guys and me. And then this other girl, Beth."

"And how was that?"

"It was a blast at first. Partying all the time. Smoking weed."

Ernestine flinched. "You mean marijuana?"

"Yeah. Like, you know, pot."

"You know that's illegal."

"Sure, but not everywhere. But yeah, it still is in California."

"You don't have any of that weed with you, do you?"

"No, don't worry. I quit doing that shit when I, like, found out I was pregnant."

"That's smart. It would be bad for the baby."

"Yeah, I know. But when I told Marcus that, he got all weird about it."

"He didn't understand it would be harmful?"

"Maybe. But he didn't care. Told me I wasn't fun anymore. He got all, like, bummed and started hanging around our pad all day getting high. Stopped, like, even trying to get work."

"So he was going to take you to see your mom?"

"Yeah, I, like, told him she'd probably let us stay till the baby comes. And I asked him to not, like, smoke while we were there. That's when he got, like, really mad."

"So Marcus dumped you because you didn't want him to smoke pot?"

"That and... well, he doesn't want the baby."

"Does your mom know you're coming?"

"No."

"Does she know you're pregnant?"

"No. I haven't, like, talked to her in six years."

Seeing tears well up in Clover's eyes, Ernestine said, "Oh, honey, I'm sorry. I'm asking too many questions."

Clover put her elbows on the table, and rested her face on her hands. The puppy crawled out from under the table, shook himself, and trotted to the cab, where he jumped up on the passenger seat beside Walter.

Ernestine felt bad about interrogating the girl but she had so many questions. Why had she really left home? Why had she lived with her dad instead of her mother? Why was her mother in New York? And why hadn't they spoken in six years? When she feels like talking,

Ernestine thought, I'll try to come up with a plan. We can probably take her at least as far as Colorado.

Even though she intended to stop quizzing the girl, Ernestine only managed to stay quiet for five minutes. "Six years is a long time. Is that when your mother left?"

Clover raised her head. "Yeah."

"And you were how old?"

"Eleven."

"That must have been hard. Not having your mom."

"Kind of. But we were good, Dad and my sister and me. Until Bonnie came."

"Bonnie? Girlfriend?"

"Uh-huh. When she, like, moved in everything changed. Dad changed. Bonnie pretty much took over. Wouldn't let us wear shorts or bathing suits. No TV. No movies. She even threw away my little sister's Barbie Dolls. Said they were, like, inappropriate."

"And your dad? Didn't he have any say in the matter?"

"That's the thing. He never said anything. Gave her permission to, like, raise us."

"How old was your sister?"

"Six."

"Does she get along with this Bonnie?"

"Yeah. She's just a little kid. She doesn't know any better."

Ernestine wondered if Clover was just being a teenager who resented being replaced. "So have you talked to your dad? Does he know where you are?"

"Yeah, I, like, called him after I got to California. I think he's glad I left though. Made things easier with Bonnie."

"And he doesn't know you're..."

"Oh no. And if Bonnie found out, she'd freak."

19

The expression Clover used caught Ernestine off guard. Freaking was exactly what she had done when her seventeen-year-old daughter, Linda, had turned up pregnant. She'd been hurt and embarrassed, and to be honest, she'd seen Linda's pregnancy as a reflection on her ability to parent. A failing grade she felt she didn't deserve. Trying to push away that memory, Ernestine stood up and opened the cabinet above the microwave. "Let's have a cup of tea, shall we?" When the microwave beeped she set the two steaming cups on the table. "What will you do now, do you think? Do you want to keep this baby?"

"Oh, God yes. I could never give my baby away."

As Ernestine sipped her tea, she recalled how differently Walter had reacted to Linda's pregnancy.

Sure, he'd been disappointed, but instead of freaking out the way she had, he'd accepted the fact and helped Linda and Matt get on their feet. He'd even given Matt a job at the store. Reminded of Walter's forgiving nature, Ernestine made up her mind to tell him about Las Vegas. What reason did she have to think he'd hold it against her?

"Clover," she said, "you sit here and finish your tea. I need to go talk with Walter." She moved to the front passenger seat, lifted the warm, sleeping puppy and put him in her lap.

Walter looked over and smiled. "Cute pup, huh? I think I'm going to like having him along."

Ernestine opened her mouth to tell him what she'd done, but the words didn't come. Not those words anyway. "We need to find a place to camp before it gets dark."

Walter nodded but didn't say anything. Ernestine knew he heard her, though, because a few miles farther on he pulled off the road amid some trees. "This will work for tonight," he said. "We'll be fine without hookups."

Once they were parked, however, he couldn't get the generator to work. And without the generator, they had no air conditioning. Ernestine pressed him to figure out what was wrong, but he balked, saying he was too tired to worry about it. It was sweltering inside the motorhome and they slept with the windows open. That didn't help, however, because it was even hotter outside.

Ernestine woke up cranky and determined to solve the generator problem. She scoured the pages of Walter's RV magazines until halfway through a long article on Basic RV Electricity she found what she was looking for.

"Walter, listen to this. The system is designed so that when the fuel tank gets down to one-quarter full, the generator will stop running. That way it doesn't use all of the fuel in the motorhome." She looked at the gas gauge, and sure enough, the needle was well below the one-quarter mark.

"I knew that," he said.

"For crying out loud," she snapped. "If you knew it, why didn't you say so last night?" Irritated, she picked up the Route 66 map she'd been looking at before. "There's only one filling station along this stretch. It's called Gas & Grub. It's the last one until we get to Seligman, which is fifty miles away." Wanting to make sure they didn't miss it, she sat forward the way she had when she was watching for deer, and scanned the roadside.

"That's it," she said pointing at the sprawling white building up ahead with its large "Gas" sign.

When he didn't slow down, she raised her voice. "Walter. We need to stop."

"Why?"

"We need gas."

"Didn't we just get gas?"

Her mouth dropped open in disbelief. "No, dammit, look at the gas gauge. We have less than a quarter of a tank. Didn't you hear what I just said about the generator? For God's sake, pay attention."

Hitting the brakes, Walter flipped a U-turn and slid up to the outermost gas pump, startling the attendant who was standing there. "Holy crap," the kid said jumping out of the way, "what happened to your rig?"

"Huh?" Walter looked at Ernestine and didn't answer.

"It looks bad, man. Ya shouldn't be drivin' it like that."

"Well I am, aren't I?"

"Okay, suit yourself, but I wouldn't."

"Who asked you?"

"Walter!" Ernestine gasped. "No need to be rude." Embarrassed, she slumped back in her seat and stared at the rolling numbers on the gas pump. The cost of the trip was already way more than she'd anticipated, and the anxiety about possible charges from Las Vegas chafed like a rash under her bra strap. The gas tank was taking forever to fill and she felt like she'd explode if she didn't find out what her credit card balance was.

"I'm going for a walk," she said. "I need to stretch my legs." Praying she could get cell reception, she headed to the far end of the building where Walter wouldn't see her, and dialed the back-home neighbor who was picking up their mail.

Mavis was thrilled to hear from Ernestine. "I've been thinking about you ever since you left," she gushed. "I'm so jealous. I bet you're just having the best time."

"It's been fun," Ernestine lied. "How are things at home?"

"Same old, same old," Mavis said. "Been awful hot. Grass is dry as sticks, but your garden is going crazy. I've been picking your tomatoes and your zucchinis—"

"Say, I'm calling about the mail," Ernestine interrupted, "is there anything that looks important?"

"Well, there's the water bill and the electric, but they aren't due for a while yet. That's about all. And, oh yeah, there's a letter from your bank. Want me to open it?"

Ernestine's hands started to shake. This is what she'd feared. She had gone over her credit limit and was in debt up to her eyeballs. "Yes, please. What does it say?"

"Dear Mrs. Emmons, Thank you for being a valued customer..."

"Skip that part. What else? Does it say how much I've gone over..."

"Over? No. It says they've increased your credit limit to ten thousand dollars."

Astonished, she let out the breath she'd been holding. Maybe she wouldn't have to tell Walter about Las Vegas after all. In fact, and this was a scary thought, maybe even if she told him, he wouldn't remember. He hadn't remembered about needing gas when she'd said it just minutes before. He seemed not to know about the damage to the RV when the kid asked him. And there was another thing, ordinarily he would have been in a big hurry to call the insurance agent and initiate the claims process and he hadn't said a word about it.

So after talking to Mavis, Ernestine called their agent, Ted Thurber at State Farm. Ted, a long-time family friend, answered the phone.

"Ted, it's Ernestine. We had an accident with the RV. Hit a deer."

"Oh no," the agent said, "Are you all right? Where are you?"

"We're in Arizona and we're not hurt. But there's some damage."

She went on to explain how it happened, and described the condition of the front end. She decided not to mention the other scrapes and scratches or the missing window, because they had nothing to do with this particular incident.

"Let me talk to Walter," Ted said. "I can explain the options about getting it fixed."

"Can't you explain it to me?" Ted knew Walter well, and Ernestine was afraid he would pick up on his fuzziness

"Well, okay, I guess that'd be all right. You'll need to locate a shop that does body work on RVs and I'm not sure—where did you say you are?"

"Arizona. We're on our way to the Grand Canyon. The motorhome runs fine. We just can't drive at night because of the headlight."

"Well, let me do some research and get back to you. I suggest you find a campground and stay there until we can get you into a repair shop. Is everything else okay?

"Yes. We're fine."

"I'll let you know when I find a place that repairs RVs. I assume you're calling from a cell phone."

"Yes. Oh wait. I don't know my number. I can't see it while I'm on the phone."

"Ernie, Ernie it's okay. The number you're calling from shows up on my phone."

"It does? Well, isn't that something? Okay, we'll wait to hear from you."

Friend or not, Ted's suggesting he talk to Walter instead of her was demeaning. She supposed, though, that it was her own fault for always stepping aside and letting Walter take charge of everything having to do with money.

When Ted called back, he said there were three State Farm preferred collision repair shops in Flagstaff. "How soon do you think you can get there? I can set it up for you if you want."

"We'll want to stay and see the Grand Canyon, so it might be two or three days."

"Can I talk to Walter?"

"He's out walking the dog right now. I'll let him know what you said."

"Okay then," Ted said. "By the way, I didn't know you had a dog."

20

When they got to Seligman, Walter picked up I-40. Ernestine tried to talk to him about finding a camp site, but he seemed distracted. She took the Good Sam book and moved to the back where Clover was curled up on the sofa. The puppy was on one side of her and the kitten was on the other. She was petting them both.

"I'm worried about Walter," Ernestine confided. "He acts like he doesn't remember hitting that deer."

"He was, like, driving when it happened, right?"

"Yes, of course. And you heard me tell him about the generator, didn't you? That it didn't work because we were low on gas?"

"Yeah, that was, like, weird. He said he didn't know why it didn't work, and then he said he knew it all along."

"And when I told him to stop for gas, he thought we already had."

"That was, like, scary, too, the way he slid into that gas station. Maybe he's just, like, tired. Do you think he's okay to drive?"

"Well, yes, he has to be."

They were about forty miles from Williams, where the junction to the Grand Canyon was, and by now Ernestine had lost interest in seeing it. She decided to not say anything and hope Walter had changed his mind. If he had, they could go straight on to Flagstaff and arrange to get the Allegro fixed.

Before reaching the junction, they started seeing billboards: SOUTH RIM BUS TOURS, HELICOPTER FLIGHTS, PINK JEEP TOURS, GRAND CANYON SKYWALK. "Look in the book," Walter said, "and find us a campsite." It was the first time he'd spoken in over an hour but obviously he hadn't changed his mind.

All the recommended campgrounds required reservations, which they didn't have, but Ernestine decided to try anyway. She called one that claimed to be within twenty-five miles of Grand Canyon National Park and pled ignorance. She said she didn't know they needed a reservation, didn't have a computer, and because her RV was missing a headlight, she was desperate. "Besides," she told the woman on the phone, "my husband is eighty years old and he's not feeling well." The woman took pity on her, and granted them a spot right next to the bathhouse.

Walter had no trouble sliding the Allegro into the narrow space between two other RVs, leaving Ernestine to wonder if she'd imagined his distraction. Maybe she was making something out of nothing, something Walter had accused her of more than once. Like Clover said, he was probably just, like, tired.

When Walter started the setup, Clover got out to help. Ernestine could hear the two of them outside, Walter telling the girl what went where and laughing with her when she did something wrong. Ernestine couldn't help wondering where that joviality was when she worked with him.

When the setup was done, Walter went about covering the headlight with duct tape. "Good as new," he said stepping aside to look at his handiwork. He'd be perfectly happy, Ernestine thought, to let the damn thing fall apart under us.

"Hey, Walt," Clover said when he was done patching the headlight, "Chip needs to pee. Do you want to walk him while I go take a shower?"

"Sure," he said, not seeming to mind Clover's sudden familiarity. "I'd like that. Where's his leash?"

Clover put the collar on the pup and watched as Walter walked him toward some trees.

"Wow," Ernestine said, "his mood sure has changed. You really have a way with him."

"He reminds me of my grandpa," Clover said digging in her backpack. Me and him always got along good." When she stood up, she was holding some folded clothes. "I'll go use that public bathhouse over there. I don't want to make a mess of your bathroom."

Ernestine was glad to hear that. The motorhome's lavatory was awfully small and the girl was awfully dirty. "Here, honey," she said, handing over a bar of soap, shampoo, conditioner, and a fingernail brush. "You'll need these."

Clover was gone for a long time and came back looking like she'd been polished. Her face and hair were shiny, her fingers and toes were pink, and she'd even managed to scrub the left-over polish from her nails. She had changed into a long flowing dress, wrinkled but clean, and she had on a fresh pair of sandals.

"You clean up good," Walter said when he came back with the dog. "Maybe we'll keep you after all." He had gone by the campground store on his walk and picked up several leaflets. "Look what I found," he said spreading a full-color brochure on the table. "I want to see this Skywalk thingy."

Clover leaned in to look and Walter winked at her. "Ernie's afraid of heights," he said, "maybe you and I could go."

"That would be awesome," Clover said. "I'd love to do that."

Ernestine glanced at the prices. "I'm not sure that's a good idea. It might not be good for the baby."

"Baby?" Walter's eyes got big like he had just now noticed Clover's belly.

"By the way, when are you due?" Ernestine asked, "Were you seeing a doctor in California?"

"Once. I went to a free clinic, but I wasn't sure about my last period so they didn't, like, give me a date."

"Big as you are, honey, you could be pretty close."

"I guess so."

While they ate dinner, they looked at the other brochures. Now that Walter was aware of Clover's condition, he turned protective. "Jeep tour would be too bumpy. Helicopter ride wouldn't be good either." Ernestine was glad to hear him say that because of how expensive the tours were.

"Why don't we just take the bus to the South Rim?" she suggested. "We can see the Grand Canyon from there."

Saying that out loud made her feel like a tightwad. The Skywalk was something Walter really wanted to do and they weren't likely to ever have another chance. It would probably be Clover's only chance, too. Besides, it wasn't true it could harm the baby. She'd only said that because of the cost. "Oh heck, let's do it. I am afraid of heights but I'll go along."

21

At the Grand Canyon visitor center, Ernestine and Clover met with a tour operator and listened to him rattle off the different tour packages and their prices. He spoke so fast that Ernestine had to lean forward and strain to grasp what he was saying. There was a Legacy Package, which included the free Hop-On-Hop-Off shuttle, but DID NOT include the Skywalk. The Skywalk was what Walter wanted to see. In order to do that you had to buy the Gold Package which appeared to include lunch.

Ernestine took a deep breath, handed over her credit card, and watched while other tourists added upgrades like professional photos, horseback rides, airplane rides, and twenty-minute helicopter tours that landed below the rim. It was insane. She couldn't believe people could afford to spend so much on one sightseeing excursion.

That evening, she spoke with the manager of the campground who'd been so accommodating, allowing them a space even though they didn't have a reservation. "We're going to take that Skywalk excursion tomorrow," she said, "is there a place we can leave the pup while we're gone?"

"We have a service for that," the woman said pointing to a small modular building. "They charge an hourly rate. They'll walk the dog and see it has water." Relieved, Ernestine went back and told Clover and Walter about the arrangement she'd made.

The next morning, while Walter and Ernestine were getting dressed, Clover took Chip to the modular. When she got back, Ernestine was standing outside, looking steamed.

"He says he's not going. Can you talk to him? He won't listen to me."

Clover stepped inside. "What's wrong, Walter? You said you wanted to see the Skywalk."

"I don't want to go. I'm staying here."

"Come on Walter. She's already got the tickets. It's the Grand Canyon. It'll be fun."

He planted himself on the bench behind the dinette table and gripped its edges. "I'm not going."

Clover went back to where Ernestine was waiting. "I can't get him to change his mind. Do you think he'll be all right here alone?"

"I've never seen him act like this, Ernestine said. "Come on, let's go or we'll miss the shuttle. He'll be fine here."

Most of the tourists on the shuttle were Japanese. There was a wiry little woman, the tour guide Ernestine supposed, who kept shouting instructions. By the time they got off the bus and were herded to the visitor center, Ernestine had figured out that tan'itsu fairu must mean single file, that isoge meant hurry, and foto gurafu meant to take pictures.

They stood as a group at the outer edge of the horseshoe-shaped bridge and Ernestine felt her legs wobble. "Oh honey," she said to Clover who was set to waddle the full seventy feet of bridge that hung out over the canyon. "I don't think I can do this."

"Sure you can, just don't look down."

As soon as Clover said that, Ernestine looked down. "Oh my God!" Beneath her feet was—nothing. She was looking straight down through clear glass to the bottom of the red-hued chasm four thousand feet below. She felt her stomach lurch.

"Come on, try," Clover said. "You paid for this. You don't want to waste another ticket, do you?"

Holding onto the railing and breathing rapidly, Ernestine slid one Nike-clad foot after the other, like a beginning ice skater afraid of falling.

"That's right," Clover urged, "you're doing good. It's gonna be, like, amazing. You're gonna love the view."

Hugging the handrail, she skated after Clover. Pressing around her were tourists from all over the world, shoving this way and that, speaking in languages she didn't recognize, and not caring who they stepped on. Some of the more vocal folks complained about not being allowed to bring cameras, while the ones who had shelled out the money for professional photos were herded ahead of those who hadn't. Ernestine felt dizzy and feared she was going to be sick.

By the time she caught up with Clover, who was standing on a bottom rail leaning well out over the edge, Ernestine was wringing wet with sweat.

"This is so awesome," Clover said leaning even farther. Just as she turned to face Ernestine, a young man pointed a camera at them.

"Smile," he said a half second before snapping their picture. He handed them a card. "You can pick up your photo on the way out."

"Wow," Ernestine said. "We didn't even have a chance to pose."

Gripping Clover's hand hard enough to leave marks, Ernestine moved closer to the edge and stood with her arm around Clover, gazing at what was in front of her. Clover was right, the view was awesome.

As they were leaving, Clover spotted their photo among the hundreds on display. In it, she looked radiant. Ernestine, on the other hand, looked like she was being tortured. There was, however, a stunning view of the canyon behind them.

"Oh my," Ernestine said, "I look awful."

"No you don't. Can we buy it? I'd really like to have something to remember you by."

Ernestine would have preferred to burn the picture, but that "something to remember you by" tugged at her heartstrings. She'd grown fond of the girl and her unborn baby and the thought of dropping her off somewhere made her sad. She really hoped Clover would be able to find another ride? Ernestine stepped up to the cashier and paid for two copies of the photo. She gave one to Clover and stuck the other one in her pocketbook. All the way back on the bus, she played with the possibility of taking Clover the whole way. How long, she wondered, would it take to get to New York?

Walter met them at the door of the motorhome. His face was red and he was clearly angry. "Where did you go?" he demanded. "I've been looking all over for you."

"What do you mean? We went to the Skywalk. You didn't want to go with us, remember?" Ernestine turned to Clover and they locked eyes.

"I didn't know where you went," Walter repeated, "I couldn't find you."

Clover stepped in front of Ernestine and patted Walter on the shoulder. "Hey, we're here now. Let's go sit down and have a cup of coffee." She led him to the dinette table and put a cup of left-over coffee in the microwave.

Puzzled by Walter's claim, Ernestine moved past the kitchen area toward the back, where she slipped on a puddle and saw the puppy cowering nearby. "Walter!

Why is the dog here? We left him with the park manager."

"I missed him, so I got him back."

"But look what's happened," she scolded. "Didn't you take him out to pee?"

Clover gave Ernestine a stern look, and she stopped. The girl was right. Yelling at him wasn't going to help. She got a towel and sopped up the mess. It wasn't Chip's fault.

It was mystifying how Walter could know where they'd left the dog, but not remember where she'd gone. When they started the trip, she had worried about him having a heart attack or hurting his back. Mental issues weren't even on her radar. Now, a couple of weeks into the trip and she was wondering if there was something wrong with his brain.

He'd said he missed the dog and now he sat, stroking the puppy's fur and apparently not remembering he'd been yelled at. Ernestine didn't understand what was happening with Walter but she could see that he had grown extremely fond of Chip. It made her think of the Golden Retriever, River, he'd had years ago. That dog had gone with him everywhere.

It was back when Walter used to go pheasant hunting, before he expanded the store and got so busy. She'd loved watching him and River together, seeing how they seemed to know exactly what the other was thinking. Even before Walter put on his jacket or picked up his keys to go somewhere, River would plant himself beside the pickup truck. Walter loved that dog so much that when it developed cancer and had to be put to sleep, he vowed to never have another dog. Ernestine sensed, now, all that unspent love being given to Chip.

22

All the next morning Ernestine's mind was on money. She had shelled out a lot on that Grand Canyon excursion and she had no idea what her credit card balance was or how to find out. More specifically, she needed to know how badly she'd screwed up at that casino. The arrangement she had with her neighbor Mavis seemed fine at first. Mavis would open the bills, tell her what she owed, and Ernestine would send the checks. But things were different now. She wasn't comfortable having Mavis see the bill from the credit card company. Mavis was, after all, a major-league gossip, and the last thing Ernestine wanted spread through the neighborhood was that she'd lost a lot of money in a gambling casino in Las Vegas.

Other than writing checks for household expenses, Ernestine had never been involved with the family finances. Walter was old-school that way, believing the man of the family should take care of the money. He handled all their major purchases and invested in the stock market. It was this investing, she knew, that allowed the purchase of the motorhome, but she didn't know how much they had or how to access it, and she couldn't bring herself to ask him.

Now she wished she had been more involved. She knew her daughter Linda handled most of her family's finances. She'd heard her talk about checking her credit card balances online, paying bills with "one click," and logging in to make changes in their investments. Ernestine didn't know how to do any of that.

Her mind was so busy with questions that she forgot all about fixing lunch until Clover offered to make sandwiches and Walter got up to help.

"Here," Clover said handing him a knife, "you spread the mayonnaise on these bread slices and I'll get the ham and cheese." She reached into the refrigerator and when she turned back, Walter was smiling proudly. He had put each pair of bread slices together and cut them in half. Clover still held the ham and cheese so there was nothing in the sandwiches but mayonnaise.

"Thank you, Walter," she said, casting a glance at Ernestine. "Why don't you go sit down and let me finish?"

After they'd eaten, Walter went to the back for a nap. Ernestine was anxious to talk with Clover out of his earshot. "Bring the puppy," she said, "let's go for a walk."

Hearing "walk," Chip, perked up his ears, jumped off the sofa, and wagged his tail so hard that Clover had to trap him between her knees to get his leash on. Outside, the puppy sniffed and peed on just about every bush they came to. "It's, like, amazing how much he can pee," Clover said. "He goes even more that I do."

"You know why I wanted to get away, don't you?" Ernestine said.

"I think so. You want to talk about Walter."

"Right. The way he made those sandwiches and didn't even notice—"

"—that the meat and cheese were missing."

"I don't know what's going on with him. It's like he's not even awake."

Clover didn't say anything.

"And yesterday. Him not remembering we'd gone to the Skywalk. After it'd been his idea to go in the first place."

Clover nodded.

"You're so good with him," Ernestine said. "I get annoyed, but you don't let any of it bother you."

"Well yeah. My grandpa had Alzheimer's. I learned from helping with him that it doesn't do any good to try to correct him. You just have to let things go."

"Oh dear, you don't think Walter..."

"Has Alzheimer's... Oh gee. I'm not saying that. There could be lots of reasons he's ... but, like, yeah, there's something."

Alzheimer's? No. It couldn't be that. Ernestine tried to push the worrisome thoughts from her head. Walter was okay. He had to be. If there was something seriously wrong, she'd know it, wouldn't she?

"Maybe being away from home has him disoriented," she said hoping that was the answer. They kept walking without either of them saying anything. Ernestine took a deep breath and switched her attention to the other thing that was worrying her. Like how much money she might have lost in the casino. By the time they got to the end of the road and turned around, she'd decided to ask Clover for help.

She held up the phone. "Um, I need to know my credit card balance. Is there a way to do it with this?"

"Sure, we can call. On the back of your card there's a number. They'll tell you your balance."

"Oh. It's that easy? I wish I'd known that."

"I'll show you when we get back."

"Good. And can you show me how to pay bills online? I know my daughter does that with her phone. Can we do that?"

"Oh sure—Chip, No!" The puppy, who'd been sniffing trees and peeing, suddenly took off after a big tan and white pit bull that was lying under the tongue of a travel trailer. Clover gave the leash a yank but Chip kept barking until she got him away from where he could see the other dog. "He doesn't know how little he is," Clover said.

When they got back to the RV, Walter was still sleeping so Ernestine got the credit card and keyed in the phone number. When prompted by the robotic voice, she entered her account number and her zip code and was amazed when the voice said, "Ernestine" and rattled off her balance of six thousand seven hundred forty-two dollars and seventeen cents, her available balance of three thousand two hundred fifty-seven dollars and eighty-three cents, and her minimum payment of thirty-five dollars, due August 20th.

She ended the call and took a deep breath. Even without a list of actual charges, it was clear that her night in the casino hadn't destroyed them. Letting that sink in, she got out a pencil and paper and did some figuring. She estimated the smaller bills she knew were coming due, the water and electricity and insurance premiums, and with that figure in mind, decided what portion of the credit card bill she would pay. It had never occurred to her that she could pay as little as thirty-five dollars.

"You young people are so good with technology," she said to Clover. "Do you mind if we set up the online banking now?"

Coming up with a password was the hardest part. Clover told her it should have at least eight characters, both letters and numbers, and should include symbols like @ or #. Ernestine thought for a long time, then handed Clover a piece of paper where she'd written, WalErn1234#. "Wal for Walter, Ern for me, and 1234."

"No. Too easy to figure out."

"Who would want to?"

"Hackers. People who, like, break into other people's bank accounts and steal their money."

"Oh dear! I never thought of that."

"So your password has to be hard."

Ernestine thought for several more minutes, then wrote, LiMa1315@.

"What's that one?"

"My daughter and her husband and the grandson's ages."

"Still too easy. How about this?" Clover handed the paper back to Ernestine. Zw23#@Yt.

"What's that mean?"

"Nothing, that's why it's good. You'll have to remember it though."

"I'll never remember that. Can I write it down someplace?"

"Yes, but don't, like, carry it in your purse."

Nervous now, Ernestine reached for the phone. "Maybe this isn't such a good idea..."

Clover pulled the phone away. "No, it's okay." She entered the password. "You just have to be careful who you, like, tell it to."

"Thank you," Ernestine said when it was all done. "I'm sure you'll have to help me when I'm ready to pay the bills. "I'll never remember all those steps."

"Sure," Clover said, "no problem."

With that taken care of, Ernestine decided to go ahead and arrange to get the motorhome fixed. She called the number the insurance agent had given her and learned the shop had already been notified about the accident and were expecting them two days ago. Good old Ted, she thought, always one step ahead of us.

23

Again, Ernestine couldn't sleep. She kept going over things in her head. Walter not remembering about the generator, forgetting she'd told him they needed gas, and how upset he got when he knew good and well she'd gone to the Skywalk.

For the first time since Walter retired, she found herself reexamining the things Leona and the other employees at his store had told her. The accounting mistakes he'd made, the supplies he'd ordered that they didn't need, and the wrong advice they said he'd given to customers. And in hindsight she recalled the things that had been happening at home. How he was always forgetting to do things around the house, how he repeated things and ask the same questions over and over again. At the time, she'd chalked it up to his lack of activity and the need for a hobby. Now that Clover had brought up Alzheimer's, that possibility had her scared to death.

She'd heard of Alzheimer's, of course. It seemed to be everywhere these days. Her friend Irma's mother-in-law had been placed in a memory care facility, and there was that nurse who used to work in her doctor's office—early onset they said. People at her church were speculating about Mildred's husband, Willard, and advertisements for drugs that claim to slow the progression were all over the TV now, too. Oh, please God, she prayed, don't let it be that.

She rolled over on her side and looked at the clock. The red digital numbers read 2:36. She wasn't going to be worth a damn tomorrow if she didn't get some sleep. She threw the sheet aside and slipped out of bed. She needed to get the Alzheimer's idea out of her head. Maybe she'd get sleepy if she read.

Tiptoeing past Clover on the sofa, she picked up the novel she'd been reading and headed for the cab. She clipped a reading light to her book, read a few paragraphs, then re-read them. Her mind was not absorbing the words. For no reason in particular, she pulled aside the curtain that covered the windshield and let her eyes scan the park. The fifth-wheel across the way had a big Husky in a kennel outside the door. Probably for protection. She wondered if Chip could scare anybody off. She turned and looked the other way, down the long row of RVs, and saw a quick movement outside one about three spaces away. Squinting, she stared harder. The dark clothing made the person hard to see, but it was definitely a man. She kept looking, trying to see what he was doing. A car driving by on the road threw a beam of light, and for a second she could make out the man's beard and stocking cap. He was pulling at the door of a motorhome. She wondered what he was doing out there at 2:30 in the morning and, if it was his motorhome, why couldn't he open the door? Convinced she was witnessing an attempted break-in, she went to the sofa and shook Clover awake.

Clover rubbed her eyes. "Something wrong?"

"There's a man..."

"A man, where?"

"Down there," she pointed, "about three spaces away. Come here, look."

Clover followed her to the front and Ernestine pulled back the curtain. "See, down there? He keeps pulling on the door like he's trying to get in."

"Maybe it's his."

"Wouldn't he have a key? Or wouldn't the people inside let him in?"

"Maybe he, like, doesn't want to wake his wife."

"No. I don't think so. I saw him when a car went by. He's a burglar, I know it. I'm calling the police."

"Are you sure you want to do that?"

Ernestine was already on the phone, giving the name of the campground, her space number, and guessing at the number of the one where she'd seen the man. "Hurry, she said. "He's trying to break in."

She and Clover stayed by the window. They saw the police car pull up, watched while the officer talked to the man, and saw the man waving his arms. Then the door opened, a woman stepped out, and the man went inside.

A few minutes later there was a knock on Ernestine's door. "Ma'am," the policeman said when she opened it. "Ordinary domestic dispute is all. The RV is his. He had a bit too much to drink and the wife wasn't going to let him in." He tipped his hat. "You get some sleep now."

Ernestine felt slightly foolish, but defended her position. "He could have been a burglar. One can't be too careful."

It was before six o'clock in the morning when the barking started. Walter came out of the bedroom in his underwear and Ernestine followed, tying the belt on her bathrobe. Chip was yipping and hopping from chair to sofa and back again. Clover was looking out the side window and trying to quiet the dog.

"What is it?" Ernestine peered out and saw a man standing about twenty feet away. "That's him!"

"Him who?" Walter asked.

"The man I called the cops on."

"You called the cops?"

"Last night."

All of a sudden, there was a loud *thunk*. Then, *thunk, thunk, thunk*. The man was throwing rocks at Walter and Ernestine's motorhome.

"What the—" Walter started for the door.

"Don't go out there," Ernestine said.

Another rock. This one hit, cracking the window. "Turn me in to the police will ya?" the man yelled. *Thunk.* "Who'da ya think you are?" *Thunk.*

"Jesus," Clover said, "we need to get out of here."

Walter was already in the driver's seat and before Ernestine could finish saying, "we're not unhooked," he had put the RV in gear and stepped on the gas. There was a ripping noise from where the electrical cord was plugged into the pole, and a squeaking sound from pulling the water and sewer connections loose. He drove forward a few feet, then slammed the gear shift into reverse and headed straight for the rock thrower.

"Walter! What are you doing?" Ernestine screamed.

"Nobody throws rocks at me."

He sped down the row of RVs until the man ducked behind some trailers and couldn't be seen, and then he turned the rig around and drove back to their campsite where the power pole was bent to a sixty-degree angle and the picnic table was overturned.

"This just isn't like him," Ernestine told Clover while they righted the table and stowed the hoses that dangled from the side of the RV. "He never used to be this quick tempered. I'm afraid he's going to give himself a heart attack."

It was early and the park management office wasn't open, so unable to report the incident in person, Ernestine pinned a note to the door apologizing for the damage to the power pole. She printed her mailing address and added, "Please let me know the cost of repairs."

Now as she watched him drive, she was struck by how much older he seemed. There were lines in his face she'd never noticed before, and there was a new stoop to his shoulders. Even his walk, she realized now, was different. He no longer had the long stride she'd admired so much.

Her mind skipped to when they met. It was in a cafe where she worked as a waitress after her first marriage broke up. The job was supposed to be temporary while she saved money to start college, but somehow the years added up and she'd stayed on, waiting tables. Walter used to come in for lunch and he always chose to sit in her section. The other girls noticed and teased her about it.

He was quite a bit older, funny, and smart. She began to look forward to seeing him and felt disappointed when he didn't show up. It was fun having him flirt with her and it was fun flirting back. They talked about a lot of things. Books, movies. He had a dog that he bragged about. And he told her he loved to dance. She remembered the first time he took her dancing, and how natural it felt. It was like they'd been dancing together for years. Letting her mind drift back to those days, she could hear the music in her head and feel Walter's hand on the small of her back.

After navigated the long driveway out of the RV Park, Walter pulled onto the interstate. "Where are we going?" he asked.

Lost in thought, Ernestine jumped. "Huh? Oh, to Flagstaff."

"Why Flagstaff?"

"We're going to get the damage fixed."

"Damage?"

She sighed. "The damage to the motorhome. Remember? From when we hit the deer."

He gave her a blank look.

"Ted recommended a place."

"Ted? Ted who?"

"Ted Thurber, our insurance agent."

Walter scratched his head.

"I called him. To report the accident."

"Dammit, Ernie, why didn't you let me do that?"

The sudden change surprised her. A minute ago he didn't know what she was talking about and now he was angry because she hadn't let him make the call. Before she could respond, Clover spoke up. "You were taking a nap, Walter, and the phone battery was low. She had to call before the phone died."

"Oh," he said. "I guess that makes sense."

What a godsend she is, Ernestine thought, she can calm him down while I only manage to aggravate him.

Clover turned to Ernestine. "If you give me the address to the repair place, I can, like, use your cell phone and get directions?"

"The phone?"

"Yeah, it has a GPS."

Ernestine didn't know what GPS stood for, but she handed Clover the phone and the piece of paper with the address, moved to the sofa and placed a pillow behind her back. From there, she could hear Clover's high pitched voice and Walter's chuckle but she couldn't make out what they were saying.

Shoving the worry aside, she leaned back and tried to focus on the scenery. What's a trip for, she asked herself, if you don't enjoy the journey? Her eyes scanned the grassy meadows, the pine trees, and the red rock ledges. It was so different from where she'd lived her whole life. There were all these intriguing formations—pinnacles, she thought they were called—that looked like cathedrals rising out of the desert. In some places, the mountains resembled enormous stacks of books. Huge boulders and long, level plateaus that appeared red and purple loomed in the distance.

Moving forward, she tapped Clover on the shoulder. "Could I have the phone? I want to take pictures. I'll give it back to you when we get closer to Flagstaff." It took her a few minutes to find the camera feature, but once she had it, she started snapping at everything that caught her eye. They approached a gigantic mountain and she began seeing blackened stumps and singed pine trees. What could have been ugly, wasn't, because mixed in with all the burn, were clumps of quaking aspen trees, and even though it was only August, some had already begun to turn gold.

Curious to know what she was looking at, she consulted the Good Sam book. "That's Kendrick Mountain," she said out loud, not really caring if Walter and Clover could hear her. "It's one of the highest peaks in the San Francisco volcanic field, and it says here that the aspen trees are the first to grow back after a fire."

She continued to read and snap pictures. After a while the white-barked aspens disappeared and the vegetation changed to juniper trees. Further on they passed through thick forests of ponderosa pines and then, as they neared Flagstaff, the snow-capped Humphrey's Peak, a jagged ancient volcano, grabbed her attention and nearly took her breath away. She didn't know how many pictures she took, or how to view them, but she felt certain Clover would show her how.

"Okay," she said, giving the phone back to Clover. "You can have it now to get directions."

"Oh, my girl here won't let me get lost," Walter said. "She really knows these roads."

"In six-tenths of a mile," a woman's voice said, "turn left onto West Forest Avenue."

Ernestine jolted. "Who was that?"

"It's the GPS. Telling us where to turn."

"It talks to you?"

"Uh-huh."

"In one point one mile, continue onto East Cedar Avenue." That voice again.

"Well I'll be damned," Ernestine said. "What will they come up with next?"

Walter kept driving, turning where he was told to turn, and seeming to think it was Clover giving the directions.

When they reached Happy Trails RV Repair, Ernestine busied herself getting their insurance information and the voluminous accident report out of the jockey box while Walter strode inside the office with his hands in his pockets. When she caught up with him, he was stumbling to explain to the man at the desk the purpose of his visit.

"We're the Emmons," Ernestine interrupted, handing the man the paperwork. "I believe our insurance agent, Ted Thurber—."

"Oh yes," the man said jumping up from his seat. "Three days ago. Let's go take a look."

Walter didn't say anything, just followed the man and Ernestine out to where the Allegro was parked.

"My name's Daryl," the man said perusing the damage. "Deer? Hit pretty hard, huh?"

"We were on Route 66," Ernestine said, "on our way to the Grand Canyon. That's why it took us so long to get here. We didn't want to miss seeing that."

Daryl nodded and scratched the stubble on his chin. "Looks like the whole front end will have to be replaced." He walked around the rear and to the other side. "Whoa!" He stopped and pointed at the crease that ran from the rear wheel through the passenger side door. "That happen at the same time?"

"No," Ernestine said, "that happened before. We hit a cement wall."

"And the window with the duct tape?"

Ernestine cringed. "My fault. A bear in Yosemite. I burned some bacon."

Daryl nodded. "This isn't all gonna be covered under one claim, you know."

"That's what I figured. That's why I didn't report it all to Ted."

"We can fix it, but I'll have to give you three separate estimates."

"Aw, don't worry about those other things," Walter said, suddenly able to speak, "Long as we can drive it."

"Not fixin' it'd be a mistake," Daryl warned. "Make one hell of difference in your trade-in value."

Walter shrugged. "Why'd I want to trade it in? We'll be taking another trip next year."

Over my dead body, Ernestine thought. Once this trip was over, she never wanted to see this motorhome again.

She knew they had a fifteen hundred dollar deductible and that it would probably apply separately to each of the three incidents, but they couldn't go home without fixing all the damage. She could just imagine what Linda would have to say.

Resolving to have Walter transfer money from their mutual funds, she told Daryl to "fix it all."

"All righty then. I'll move her around to the back and get you some figures." Daryl reached for the door. "May I?"

"Wait," Ernestine said, "there's a gir—."

Daryl opened the door and was met by a growling puppy bravely defending a very pregnant girl. He turned to Ernestine. "Ted told me you two were traveling alone."

"As far as he knows, we are."

After Daryl inspected the motorhome and gave them an estimate, Ernestine asked about a loaner car. They were offered a pea green Kia.

"Way too small," she said. "We need something bigger."

"Okay, I can see that." Daryl scratched his stubble again. "Do you see something out there that'd work better?"

Before she could respond, Walter said, "That red one over there. That Hummer."

"Uh, what about a nice roomy sedan?"

"Nope," Walter's gaze was fixed on the Hummer. "We'll take that one."

Twenty minutes later, Ernestine was using the Hummer's grab bar to pull herself up to the passenger seat. "Good grief," she said, "it feels like an Army tank."

Walter turned the key and the engine thundered to life. Clover, in the back seat, clamped her arms around the cat and puppy to keep them from trying to flee.

"I've always wanted one of these," Walter hollered over the roar.

"Oh, really?" Ernestine hollered back, "I thought you always wanted a Corvette."

"Well I did. But I wanted one of these too."

The engine noise was deafening. Ernestine cupped her hands around her mouth. "Daryl said the repairs will take a couple of weeks. We need to find a motel. One that takes pets. We'll get a separate room for Clover."

"Listen," Clover called from the back seat, "you don't need to worry about me. I can find another ride."

Ernestine turned and patted Clover's knee. "Oh, no. You stay with us. At least till we get to Colorado."

24

The motel was a big step up from the last place, if she didn't count the Trump Hotel. Relieved now that she hadn't exceeded her credit limit, Ernestine felt comfortable paying for a family suite. There were two rooms plus a shared common area with a couch, table and chairs, and a desk.

"I hope you don't plan to sit here and do nothing the whole time," Walter said while Ernestine put the things she'd brought from the motorhome into dresser drawers. "I want to do some sightseeing."

"What is it you want to see this time?" Ernestine asked still annoyed about what happened at the Grand Canyon. "I don't want to get something all set up and have you change your mind. That stunt you pulled the last time ended up being expensive."

"Oh, don't go getting on your high horse. I didn't go with you because I didn't like the looks of that bus driver."

"You didn't even see the bus driver."

"Yes I did. Skinny little mama's boy with a squeaky voice."

"You didn't even see him," she repeated. "You weren't there."

"Skinny kid. Squeaky voice."

Where was this coming from, she wondered. Had he dreamt it? Was he just making things up?

"I want to see Sedona." Walter picked up a magazine from the table in their room. "Here, look at this. It's called the Chapel of the Holy Cross. It's built right into the rock."

Ernestine sat down and let him show her the pictures. "Oh my, I wonder how they did that."

"Let's drive down there."

Weary of being on the road, Ernestine thought how nice it would be to stay in one place for a while. Maybe catch up on the news. She didn't have a clue what was going on in the world.

"Why don't we stay put for a day or two? I haven't done laundry since before we got to the Grand Canyon." She expected Walter to argue, but instead he started fiddling with the TV and seemed to forget all about Sedona.

Once Clover had settled into her part of the suite, she joined Walter and Ernestine in the common area.

Ernestine handed her the phone. "Why don't you Google for a nice restaurant?"

"How does Ralph's Steak House sound?" Clover said after a few minutes. "It has four stars."

Walter stood up and turned off the TV. "That sounds good. Let's go."

The restaurant turned out to be one of those dark, rustic places with plain pine booths, low lights, and walls covered with Old West movie posters. Walter pointed out the actors as they walked past. "John Wayne, Errol Flynn, Gary Cooper, Randolph Scott…" Clover said she'd never heard of any of them except maybe John Wayne.

Once they were seated, a waitress brought menus and asked about drinks. Walter ordered a large glass of beer. Ernestine ordered wine.

"Everything looks so good," Ernestine said studying the menu. "What do you want, Walter?"

"Give me a minute."

"Clover," Ernestine asked, "What looks good to you?"

"I'm not really that hungry…"

"Nonsense," Walter said looking up from his menu, "You're hungry."

The waitress returned, and Walter hadn't decided, so Ernestine asked for a few more minutes. When five minutes later he still hadn't decided, Ernestine and Clover placed their orders.

"And you?" The waitress stood looking at Walter.

"Well … uh … give me a minute."

The waitress tapped her foot and chewed on her pencil.

"Walter?" Ernestine prompted, reaching across the table and pointing at the picture of grilled salmon with rice and fresh vegetables.

"No." He swatted her hand away. "I'll have the New York steak."

"Remember what that doctor said about red meat."

The waitress lifted her pencil and looked at Ernestine.

"And give me fries and onion rings."

"No, Walter, you'll be up all night with heartburn,"

"Leave me be!" he snapped. "I know what I want."

Stung by his insolence, Ernestine backed off, unwrapped her silverware, and took a sip of her wine. Walter fiddled with the condiments, the salt and peppers shakers, the napkins, and squirmed like a fidgety child.

"Why is it taking so damn long?" he barked.

"Shhhh!" Ernestine hissed. "She just now took our orders." She looked around the room hoping no one else had heard him. All but two of the tables were occupied. Directly across from them, an elderly couple was already eating, and up ahead was a family with two small children.

Walter downed his beer and called the waitress over. "Bring me another one."

"I don't think—" Ernestine started. Walter glared at her, so she didn't finish.

"Where the hell is my food?" he demanded when the girl brought the beer. "Did your cook go home or something?"

Ernestine winced. The young mother looked over and put her arm protectively around her little girl.

"I'll bet our order will be next." Clover said, laying her hand on Walter's.

He smiled. "Okay, sure. It'll be next."

Ernestine gulped down what was left in her wine glass. As grateful as she was for Clover's ability to calm him, it annoyed her that Walter so obviously preferred taking direction from her.

When the food arrived, he dove in as if he were starving. Clover finished her burger and reached for one of Walter's French fries. "Go ahead," he said sliding the plate in her direction, "help me out."

"No thanks," she said. "I just wanted a taste."

"Oh here, I'll help." Ernestine reached for Walter's fries, and he jabbed her with his fork.

"Ow! Walter, why'd you do that?"

"I'm not finished."

That, too, was something he'd never done before. They had always shared in restaurants, tasting each other's food, him finishing what she couldn't. She looked away and tried to pretend her feelings weren't hurt.

When the waitress brought the check, Ernestine put her credit card in the folder, scribbled on the bill, "Sorry he was rude," and added a sizable tip.

On the way out, Walter stumbled and bumped against several of the other tables. Ernestine thought she heard whispering, and she couldn't remember ever feeling more embarrassed. Dropping back a step, she took Clover's arm and whispered. "He's had too much to drink. We can't let him drive."

"Yeah, I know."

"Do you think you could?"

Clover looked at her sideways, "What? Drive?"

"Yes, it's not far."

"Why don't you?"

"I'd just rather you do it. He'll get mad if I say anything but he won't argue with you."

"Okay," Clover said, "I'll try, but I've never, like, driven a Hummer before." When they reached the door, Clover took Walter's arm. "Mind if I drive back? I've always wanted to drive a Hummer."

"Oh sure, honey," he said fishing in his pocket for the keys, "let's see what you can do."

Clover climbed awkwardly onto the driver's seat, grunted, and adjusted the mirrors. "Okay," she said, "here we go."

All the way back to the motel, Walter belched and complained, berating Ernestine for letting him eat so much.

"I tried to tell you, but you went right ahead."

"Can't you give me something?" He said, releasing a long disgusting "buuuurrrp."

"You did it to yourself, you know. I told you not to eat all that but..."

"Do you have anything to give me?"

"Just hold on till we get back to the room."

Convinced it was just indigestion, Ernestine gave him a couple of Rolaids tablets, but he'd barely gotten them in his mouth when he grabbed his chest. "Do something," he said, "I'm having a heart attack." Alarmed, Ernestine got the bottle of nitro glycerin tablets the ER doctor had given them. But if it's only heartburn, she thought, giving him nitro glycerin might be dangerous. She grabbed the phone and called 911.

"Where is the pain located?" the dispatcher asked.

"He's holding his chest."

"Ask him if he feels it in his arm and jaw."

"Your arm? Your jaw?"

He shook his head.

"He says no."

"Did you give him... before the dispatcher could finish asking the question, there was a massive rumbling sound.

"Awwwwww," Walter said, "that felt so good."

"I'm sorry," Ernestine said suppressing the urge to strangle him. "I guess it wasn't a heart attack after all."

25

For the next several days, Walter sucked on Rolaids and complained about his indigestion. It seemed he'd gotten the message about watching what he ate and insisted that now he was going to eat nothing but carrots and celery. Ernestine knew that wasn't going to last long, but she did pick up some of both at a close-by market, along with some Lean Cuisine type TV dinners. But when she offered them as an alternative to going out to restaurants, he insisted he'd never said anything about cutting back. Frustrated, she gave up and let him eat what he wanted.

Two days went by before Walter brought up Sedona again. Ernestine had woken to find him fiddling with the motel coffee maker trying to figure out where to put the water. Kissing his cheek, she deftly removed the pot from his hand and filled the tank. While the coffee pot sputtered, he sat at the table and picked up the Arizona magazine. "Have you seen this?" he said holding it out to her. "This is the Chapel of the Holy Cross in Sedona. It's built right into the rock."

Ordinarily she would have responded with, "of course I've seen it," or "you already showed it to me, don't you remember?"

"Oh my," she said, "I wonder how they did that."

"This is one of the places I want to go," he said.

"Okay, why don't you make a list of places? Maybe we'll go to Sedona tomorrow."

Walter got up and started digging in Ernestine's pocketbook. "Do you have a...a...a...thing you write with in here?"

"Here, give it to me." Ernestine took the bag from him and found a pen and a notepad.

When he was done scribbling, he handed her the paper. He'd written several things, but she could barely make them out. It was the first time she noticed how poor his handwriting had gotten.

The motel's continental breakfast had become Walter's favorite part of the day. It was a substantial buffet with everything from scrambled eggs and oatmeal to cook-your-own waffles, and having forgotten all about altering his diet, he wolfed down huge portions bubbling with enthusiasm about the day-trip to Sedona.

"Get the camera ready, Ernie," he said, "this is going to be a beautiful drive."

It was Ernestine's idea to stop at the Oak Creek Vista Point south of Flagstaff, and after reading the posted sign, she said, "Let's not do this. Let's turn back."

"Why would we do that?"

"Read the sign. It says we'll be heading into a series of switchbacks that drop forty-five hundred feet in fourteen miles. That's crazy."

"Oh, that's nothing."

Still traumatized by the horrible Tioga Pass where they'd had to take the runaway truck ramp, she proposed they go back and sign up for a tour with a bus company instead.

"Hell no. We're not taking a bus. We're here, we're going to go to Sedona."

Seeing how scared Ernestine was, Clover stepped in. "Why don't I ride up front with him? That way you won't, like, have to watch the road. We'll be all right."

Not convinced, but knowing Walter wasn't going to change his mind, Ernestine got in the back seat with the pup and the kitten, and pulled her seatbelt as tight as she could get it. Walter took the curves slowly at first, and then as he got in what he called his "rhythm," he started going faster, all the while rubber-necking the red rocks and towering outcroppings in the distance. When he turned around to ask Ernestine if she was getting pictures, he hit loose gravel and slid so far right that the front wheel actually left the roadway. Ernestine's scream was so loud and so sudden that it caused him to jerk the wheel back, side-swiping the rock wall on the inside curve. When they stopped, neither Ernestine nor Walter seemed able to speak.

Clover broke the silence. "Ernie, you're going to have to drive."

"No, Clover. I can't."

"What do you mean you can't?"

"I just can't"

"You have a driver's license, right?"

"Yes, but I can't drive this thing. Can't you do it? You drove it once before."

"I did it once, but Ernie, look at me. I'm huge. I barely fit behind the steering wheel and my feet are swelled up like balloons."

"I know, and I'm sorry, but I can't do it."

"Why not? It's not that bad if you take it slow."

"Because I'm scared. Of big vehicles. Of mountain roads. I had an accident once. Driving my brother's truck. My brother was hurt. Bad. Big rigs terrify me."

"Wow, and this Hummer isn't nearly as big as the motorhome. Why did you, like, get something that big if you were scared? Didn't you think you might have to drive it?"

"I told him I was afraid. That I wouldn't drive it. But he insisted nothing was going to happen to him. And, well... he had his heart set on it."

Clover took a deep breath. "Okay, Ernie, I'll do this, but I won't drive the motorhome." She waddled around the car and hoisted her heavy body onto the driver's seat. She adjusted the seat backwards to make room for her belly, but then her feet barely reached the pedals, so she moved it forward again pinning herself tightly between it and the steering wheel. Squirming uncomfortably, she eased the Hummer back onto the roadway. "Honestly, Ernie," she said, "you have to, like, get over it. You can't let Walter drive. And I can't either. The baby could come any time."

"He'll be fine after this," Ernestine said, more to convince herself than anything. "He just got distracted by the scenery." Even though she felt bad about making Clover do the driving, she managed to relax enough to look around and snap pictures of the things Walter pointed at.

Sedona was as beautiful as advertised. Ernestine gawked open-mouthed at all the rock formations and was so fascinated by the Chapel of the Holy Cross that she took shots of it from every angle. Walter, who had wanted to see Sedona, seemed far less impressed. After driving around for an hour, Clover parked the Hummer in the center of downtown, and the three of them strolled in and out of the art galleries and gift shops.

There was so much to look at that Ernestine failed to notice how unsteady Walter's gait was. She went about picking things up and putting them down again, eventually deciding on tee shirts for her grandsons, Jack and Jeremy. One had a picture of a cactus and said "Sedona." The other one had a skeleton lying face down on the ground and the words, "It's a dry heat."

Leaving the shops, Ernestine practically stumbled over a woman selling silver and turquoise jewelry from a blanket on the sidewalk. She apologized and stayed to browse, choosing a necklace for Linda, and bracelet she thought would look lovely on Clover.

When they'd seen enough and gone back to where the Hummer was parked, Clover opened Google maps on the iPhone. "I think there's another way back to Flagstaff," she said. "It looks like we can take I-17. It's longer by, like, twenty miles. But it's interstate. Not so scary."

"Oh thank God," Ernestine said.

Clover smiled, admiring her bracelet. "Thank you so much for this," she said. "No one has ever been so nice to me before."

It was a long drive back and it had gotten dark. Ernestine, no longer nervous about hairpin turns, was fighting sleep.

"There's something I need to tell you," Clover said out of the blue. "You know those times when I had your cell phone?"

Shaking off her drowsiness, Ernestine scooted forward and put her cheek against the back of the passenger seat so she could hear over the rumbling engine. "Yes."

"I went on Facebook. I was, like, curious, you know, to see what my ex-roommates were doing."

"Oh, that's all right. I don't mind."

"Well, like, I really just wanted to check up on Marcus."

"And?"

"I was right. He's with Beth."

"Beth?"

"The chick he was messing around with before I got pregnant."

"Is that what you wanted to tell me?"

"Well, no. I wanted to tell you I lied to you."

"Lied? About what?"

"About Marcus kicking me out at that place in Arizona. He didn't. It was me. I ditched him. I, like, hid in that Hackberry Store till he left. I didn't want him to find me."

"Why?"

"Because he was doing coke."

Ernestine gasped. "Coke? You mean cocaine?"

Clover nodded. "While he was driving. I was scared."

"I certainly understand that! What were you planning to do? After you ditched him?"

"I dunno. What I did, I guess. Get a ride and try to make it to my mom's."

"You're planning to stay with her then?"

"Yeah, if she'll have me."

"You mean because you're pregnant?"

"Well partly."

Ernestine remembered how upset she'd been when Linda got pregnant at seventeen. Still, she would have taken her in in a heartbeat.

"Of course she'll have you. She's your mother."

Pushing that memory aside, she went back to asking questions. "How did that feel, seeing Marcus on Facebook? With that other girl?"

"Awful. He's, like, such an asshole!" Clover's voice sounded thick, like she was crying.

Ernestine reached over the seat and squeezed Clover's shoulder. "Sometimes people aren't who we think they are." She felt sad for the girl who, as far as she knew, had no way to take care of a baby on her own. Sure, she'd gotten herself into this fix, but what were her choices now? Of course her mother would take her in. How could she not?

Except for the engine and Walter's snoring, there were no other sounds. "Were you and your mom on good terms?"

"Well, yeah I guess. I mean I was only eleven the last time I saw her. We didn't fight or anything. I think she was mostly mad at my dad."

"Well, I'm sure she'll be thrilled to have you with her." Ernestine leaned back against the seat next to Walter and hoped what she said was true.

26

Tired from the trip, they slept late, and since the motel's continental breakfast ended at nine o'clock, Ernestine suggested they walk to the coffee shop down the street.

"I'll go wake Clover," she said, crossing the common area and knocking on Clover's bedroom door. When she got no answer, she knocked again. "Clover, honey, you awake?" Getting no response, she opened the door. "Clover?" The room was empty. The bed was made, the backpack was gone, and there was no sign of the girl or the puppy.

She rushed back to Walter. "She's not there! Clover isn't there."

At first he didn't seem to understand what she was saying. Then, "Who? The girl? Where is she? Where's the puppy?"

"That's what I'm trying to tell you. They're gone."

Ernestine grabbed her pocketbook and headed out the door leaving Walter half-dressed and looking confused. Outside, she turned around several times before deciding to go toward the City Center rather than away from it. As she walked, her head buzzed with questions about why Clover would take off without saying anything. She picked up her pace. There weren't any sidewalks and the roadside was uneven. Her feet started to hurt and she was short of breath. When she was younger she'd enjoyed walking, but that was before she'd put on so much weight, and before her knee surgery.

Finally realizing how pointless it was to chase after the girl, she slowed down. If Clover wanted to go it alone, that was her decision to make. Disappointed and mopping her forehead with a hanky, Ernestine collapsed onto a bench in a bus shelter and was startled by a wet nose against her knee. "Chip!"

At the other end of the bench, hunched over her backpack, was Clover with her big belly and swollen ankles. For a long time, neither of them spoke. Then Ernestine asked, "Why?"

Clover sniffed. "You've got enough trouble with Walter. And you've done way too much for me already."

"If you think you're a burden, you're wrong," Ernestine said, her voice breaking with emotion. "You have no idea how much help you've been."

Tears streaked Clover's cheeks. "I didn't expect you to, like, change your whole entire trip for me."

"I know that."

Clover's eyes blazed with purpose. "But you are... you have... changed it."

Ernestine was quiet for a moment. "What will you do?"

"I'll call my dad. See if he'll, like, send me some money."

"Do you think he will?"

"I dunno."

"Come back with me, please. We want you with us."

Clover wiped at her nose with her sleeve. "Are you sure?"

"Please," Ernestine said again.

The walk back took a long time with the puppy dancing around their feet and Ernestine stopping every couple of blocks to catch her breath.

"Where's Walter?" Clover asked.

"Oh, gosh," Ernestine said, suddenly feeling a wave fear. "I left him in the room. We need to hurry."

As soon as they got to the motel, Clover handed the puppy's leash to Ernestine and launched herself up the flight of stairs. Returning to where Ernestine was waiting, she said, "He's not there."

Ernestine started for the parking lot. Then, satisfied that he hadn't taken the Hummer, she inquired at the motel office, checked the swimming pool, and even looked in the weight room. By then she was in a panic.

"Has he wandered before?" Clover asked.

"Wandered? No. Not without telling me he was going."

"You stay here with Chip," Clover said. I'll go look for him. Give me the phone just in case."

Ernestine spent the next forty-five minutes in a cold sweat, admonishing herself. What kind of person goes off without thinking about her husband? Shouldn't she have cared more for his whereabouts than Clover's? If something has happened to him, she thought, I'll never forgive myself.

She was watching out the window when Walter and Clover appeared in the parking lot. Leaving the dog, she hurried down the stairs to meet them.

"Thank God, you're all right," she said giving him a hug. "Where were you? Where did you go?"

He didn't say anything.

"I found him sitting on a bench about six blocks from here," Clover said. "He said he was looking for me and couldn't, like, remember how to get back home. He called it home."

Relieved but shaking, Ernestine led Walter back to their suite. Ordinarily she would have scolded him for scaring her, but the blank look in his eyes stopped her. This wasn't the Walter she'd been married to for forty-two years. When he lay down on the bed, she covered him with a blanket, pulled the shades, and went to Clover's room.

"I've never seen him like this," she said. "He's never gotten lost before. It's just not like him at all."

"My grandpa wandered off and got lost. It happened more than once."

"Your grandpa had Alzheimer's, right?"

"Yeah."

"Is that why your dad placed him in memory care? Because he wandered?"

"Well, that and a lot of other things."

"Where was your grandma, couldn't she take care of him?"

"She, like, died before that. Dad says the stress of taking care of Grandpa is what killed her."

Ernestine stood and gave Clover a hug. "Thanks for finding him today. I'm real sorry about your grandfather, but Walter doesn't have Alzheimer's. He's just a little confused. And anyway, I could never put him in one of those places."

"Sometimes," Clover said, "people have to."

The weeks in the motel were wearing. Except for his forgetfulness, Walter was generally fine during the day, especially after he'd eaten breakfast, but come evening he got anxious and irritable. He would get up and pace, unable to articulate what was bothering him. Ernestine tried to get him to sit down, to watch TV or play a game of checkers with her, but nothing worked. She blamed his restlessness on lack of exercise, but she couldn't get him to use the motel's exercise room or the swimming pool. At home she would have encouraged him to take walks, but given what had just happened, she didn't dare do that.

27

It was a morning in the beginning of the third week when Ernestine found Clover in the common area of their adjoining rooms sitting cross-legged on the carpet, holding her belly with both hands and looking scared.

"What's wrong?" Ernestine asked.

"I don't know. I have...What does labor feel like?"

"Well...uh, cramping...in your abdomen or your back."

"It's on the side mostly." Clover winced. "Uh! Really tight."

"Here, let's get you up on the sofa." Ernestine helped Clover up and put a pillow behind her back. "How long has it been happening?"

"Since about five. Woke me up."

"Your water hasn't broken?"

"Water?"

"Yes, honey. The sac the baby is in is filled with water. Often times that breaks when you start labor. You'll know when that happens."

"I'm scared."

"I know. But you'll be fine. I'm going to wake Walter and we'll take you to the hospital. You might not be in labor, but we'll see what's going on."

Walter got up, sluggish and disoriented. "Hospital? Who?"

"It's Clover. She might be in labor. Can you drive?"

"Of course I can drive. Why are we going to the hospital?"

"Just get dressed. Please. I'll explain on the way."

Walter came out of the bedroom, shirt inside-out, pants unzipped. "Why are we going to the hospital?"

Ernestine zipped his pants and tucked her worry away. Right now she needed to take care of Clover. "Are they letting up at all?" she asked.

"Maybe a little."

"If it is the real thing, they'd be regular, and they'd be getting stronger."

Ernestine threw a motel blanket around Clover and walked her out to the Hummer. "I saw a 24-hour Urgent Care clinic a couple blocks from here," she said after settling Clover in the back seat. To Walter she said, "Let's go there instead. They'll be able to tell if she's in labor."

He started the Hummer and pulled onto the street. It was just getting light and there was almost no traffic. Ernestine told him when to turn and where to park. She got out and led the girl into the clinic, with Walter trailing behind. While Clover was being attended to, Ernestine filled out paperwork, and because the girl had no insurance she knew of, put her own name down as the responsible party.

The technician who checked Clover assured her that her discomfort was likely Braxton-Hicks contractions and not true labor. "I strongly suggest you get an ultrasound. Today if possible. I'll have the receptionist set up an appointment."

Clover took the appointment card and stuck it in her purse. "The doctor at that place in California wanted me to get one, too, but I didn't have the money."

"I don't want you worrying about that," Ernestine said. "We're keeping the appointment."

Do you want to know your baby's sex?" the technician asked as she applied the lubricating jelly to Clover's belly.

"Yes," Clover said, grinning and squeezing Ernestine's hand. "My gram, here, and me, we're going to go shopping for baby clothes. We, like, need to know what color to buy."

They'd been planning all morning, Ernestine making a list of things she called a layette: diapers, onesies, blankets, bibs, burp cloths... Clover said she had no idea a baby needed so many things.

"You see that?" The technician moved the scanner back and forth. "There," she pointed to the screen. Clover wasn't sure what she was seeing. "There," the technician said again, "that's a penis."

"Oh my God," Clover whispered. "Oh my God. A boy. Ernestine, look, it's a boy."

"Did you say you haven't seen a doctor?" The technician asked, wiping the lubricant from Clover's belly and pulling down her shirt.

"I went to a clinic, like, one time, but my boyfriend got so mad, I didn't go back."

"Mad? Why?"

"Because I wouldn't get rid of it like he wanted me to."

That was the first time Ernestine had heard that, but somehow she wasn't surprised.

"I think you're very close to term," the technician said. "I'm guessing no more than three weeks."

"You know," Clover said, "I never, like, thought about it being a boy." She started to sing, "I have a su-*un*. I have a *son*. *I* have a son. This is my *son*! I can hardly wait to tell Walter."

All Ernestine could do was smile. It was so nice to see Clover happy. She hoped the happiness would last and that things would work out with the girl's mother. Surely she and the baby would be better off with their real family.

That evening, after Clover went to bed, Ernestine opened her door and looked in. Clover was sleeping on her side with a pillow supporting her belly, and the puppy curled up against her back. Ernestine shook her head at how young and vulnerable Clover was.

"What are you doing?" Walter asked from in front of the TV.

Ernestine pulled the door closed. "Watching her sleep. She's such a child. Walter, how far is it to New York?"

"New York?"

"Yes, that's where Clover's mother is?"

"Why would you want to go to New York?"

It was no use asking him. He wasn't going to be any help. She got the atlas and looked at the full map of the United States. She knew New York was clear on the other side of the country, but she'd never been good at geography and had no idea how big the country actually was. There was a graph that showed distances. Flagstaff to New York City was twenty-three hundred and twelve miles! That was three times as far as they'd come since leaving home. Was it even possible, she wondered, to get there in three weeks? Feeling panicky, she stood up and paced. She wished she could talk to Walter. Have him help her figure things out. But he didn't seem able to grasp anything anymore. His mind wasn't... well, it wasn't what it used to be, and it seemed to be getting worse. What a mess...A girl almost nine months pregnant and a man losing his mind...no, she was the one who would have to figure this out.

She slept badly and got up before sunrise to watch the numbers on the clock creep toward when the body shop opened. At six fifty-five, she went to the bathroom. At six fifty-eight, she pulled out the card with the number of the repair shop. When the digits rolled over to seven, she dialed.

"Happy Trails RV Repair! How may I help you?" The woman who answered sounded sleepy. Like she hadn't had her first cup of coffee.

"This is Mrs. Emmons," Ernestine said, "You have our Allegro. I need to know when it'll be ready." She was put on hold for what seemed like forever.

"Mrs. Emmons," the gruff male voice startled her. "I know we've had your vehicle for nearly three weeks now and you've been very patient, but we're still waiting for parts. Hopefully the end of next week. I promise I'll keep you posted."

Well, Ernestine thought, that was that. She'd been counting on getting Clover home before the baby was born, but now that seemed impossible. The best she could do was buy Clover a bus ticket and pray things would work out with her mom.

It was almost an hour later, when Ernestine knocked on Clover's door. "Come in," Clover called sleepily.

"We need to talk," Ernestine said, going in and making herself comfortable on the edge of Clover's bed.

"Is something wrong?"

"Well yes, and I couldn't feel worse about it."

"Did I do something?"

"Of course not, no." She smoothed Clover's blond hair and tucked a strand behind her ear. Saying goodbye to this girl was going to be harder than she thought. "I was hoping we could take you all the way to your mom's before the baby comes. I wanted to see you settled. Meet your mom and make sure you were going to be all right."

"I know, and I can't tell you how much —"

"But, honey, we're not going to make it. It's over two-thousand miles to New York, and you've got less than three weeks. It's going to be at least a week before the motorhome is fixed, so...I'm so sorry."

Clover looked puzzled. "New York?"

Ernestine frowned. "Where your mother is."

"My mother? In New York?"

"Why yes. You said..."

"Ohhhhh." Clover started to laugh. "You thought...You thought...my mom was... Oh," she grabbed the sides of her belly "in New York?"

"Isn't that where you said she lived? In Manhattan?"

Gasping for breath, Clover said, "Manhattan. Manhattan, *Kansas*. My mom *hated* big cities. She lives in Manhattan, *Kansas*."

Once Ernestine caught on to what had just happened, she started to laugh too.

28

The shopping trip to Walmart started out fun. Walter was even more excited than Clover and Ernestine. He kept adding things to the cart the way a toddler picks cereal off grocery store shelves. Ernestine followed behind him, putting them back and replacing them with things she thought more appropriate. Clover swooned over the adorable baby outfits but kept insisting that Ernestine and Walter were giving her too much.

"You'll need plenty of these." Ernestine dumped six large packages of Pampers in the cart and moved to the aisle with the bottles, pacifiers, and nursing supplies. "I haven't asked, but will you be breastfeeding your baby?"

"You mean, like, natural?"

"Yes. Have you thought about it?"

"Sort of. But doesn't it ruin your figure?"

"Oh, no. Just the opposite. You'll get your shape back sooner if you breastfeed."

"But I thought..."

"Did someone tell you that?"

"My mom. After my sister was born. Her and dad had a fight about it. She said it would ruin her figure, and he said she wasn't a high-school beauty queen anymore and should start acting like a mother."

"So your mom was a beauty queen?"

"Yeah, I guess. Her and Dad met in high school. He was a big-time jock."

"How about you? Did she nurse you?"

"I doubt it. She was always into what she looked like. Always worrying about her figure and her hair. I don't think she liked being a mom. She was always saying things like, 'This isn't what I signed up for.' I took care of my baby sister, Willow, more than mom did."

"Really? How old were you when your sister was born?"

"Five. Mom got mad when Willow cried, so I learned how to fix bottles and change her diapers. Learned how to keep her from crying."

Ernestine listened in disbelief. No wonder the poor girl thought her mother wouldn't want her.

"But I'm going to be a good mom. I am."

"I believe you will be," Ernestine said.

"Did you nurse your baby?" Clover asked.

"Yes I did. It's the best way to give babies a healthy start. But the biggest benefit is how it allows you to bond with your baby. And you know what else? It's a lot cheaper than buying formula." Ernestine picked up a package of nursing pads and some lanolin cream and turned to throw them in the cart, but it was gone. And so was Walter.

"For crying out loud," she said, "where did he go now?"

Clover waddled toward men's wear, shoes, bedding, and sporting goods. Ernestine went in the other direction, toward groceries and cleaning supplies, and was about to panic and call store security when she saw Clover waving to her from the rear of the store. Hardware. Relieved, she walked as fast as she could to where Clover was pointing. The shopping cart full of baby things sat near an "Employees Only" door, and Walter was standing behind the hardware counter.

"Walter," Ernestine hissed, "Come out of there. You're not supposed—"

"Let me," Clover said going up to where Walter was fiddling with the cash register. "Excuse me," she said, "can you help me find a hammer?"

Walter's face brightened but showed no recognition. "This way. It'll be right over here."

Ernestine watched in disbelief as he walked off with Clover, explaining, the way he had when he worked in his store, the different types of hammers and their uses. Shocked and shaken, but trusting Clover to handle Walter, Ernestine retrieved the shopping cart and went to the front of the store to check out. In the parking lot, she loaded her purchases into the Hummer and leaned against its side, wondering what in hell was going to happen next.

Clover came out of the store, leading Walter by the hand.

"Where are we going?" he asked.

"Back to the motel."

"I can't. I'm working."

"Your shift is over. It's time to go home."

"Oh, that's right," he said opening the door of the Hummer and climbing in the driver's seat. He started the engine. "Come on, Linda," he said, "get in."

Ernestine looked at Clover, raised her eyebrows, and mimed, "Linda?"

On the way out of the parking lot, Walter missed the stop sign and nearly collided with a car coming in. Then, instead of turning left, he went right.

"It's the other way," Ernestine said.

"I know where it is," he snapped.

"It *is* the other way," Clover said.

Walter flipped a U-turn in the middle of the block, clipped the concrete divider and bumped down onto the other side of the street.

"Holy crap," Clover gasped. "I would have waited till we got to the corner."

Luckily, the motel was only another three blocks and Walter recognized the big Best Western sign. As soon as he parked, Clover grabbed a few packages, got out, and made a beeline for their rooms. She used the key-card, dropped the packages on the floor, and ran to the bathroom. When she came out, Chip was sitting on his haunches with a playful look in his eyes.

181

"Wuf. Wuf." A pair of tiny socks lay on the floor in front of him. Clover reached for them, but Chip was too fast. He grabbed the socks in his teeth.

"Give it." Clover said holding out her hand. Chip backed up and wagged his tail. Clover reached again. "Drop it." He backed up more. "Okay, you want to play?" She grabbed the socks, but Chip's teeth were clamped, and he pulled. She let go and turned her back, and he dropped the socks. She spun around and reached again, but Chip was quicker. With the socks in his teeth, he stared at her, daring her to get them. His tail was wagging like crazy. When Clover walked away and ignored him, he dropped the socks. "You silly dog," she said, petting his silky ears. "I don't know how I'm going to take care of you and a baby."

Meanwhile, the kitten was pouncing on the packages of Pampers, getting her claws stuck in the plastic, ripping them out and pouncing again. Dealing with the playful pets and putting the packages out of reach were temporary distractions, and it wasn't until Walter had gone to lie down that Ernestine had a chance to talk to Clover about what had happened at Walmart.

"He must have thought he was back at his old job," Ernestine said. "He owned a hardware store you know."

"I didn't know that. So, like, that makes sense. That's why he was behind the counter and trying to run the cash register."

"You handled him so well. I just wanted to yell at him. Tell him to get out of there."

"I know, but you can't, like, do that. Arguing makes things worse. You have to play along. Did you hear him call me Linda? That's your daughter's name, right?"

"Yes, he must have you confused with her."

"You know, Ernie, the way he drove coming back here. You can't let him keep driving. What if he has an accident?"

"He loves to drive."

"That U-turn he did today, that was scary! All I know is, if he, like, has an accident and they find out he has...whatever he has...you'll get sued big time."

"Did your grandpa drive?"

"He did until Dad told the DMV about the Alzheimer's. Then they took his license away. He was super pissed, but at least he didn't blame Dad."

Ernestine put her head in her hands. "Walter would be furious. I know he would. Dammit, none of this was supposed to happen. This whole trip was his idea. He was the one who wanted to buy an RV. He was the one who wanted to travel and see the national parks. I told him when we bought the motorhome that I wouldn't drive it."

"But you'll have to, Ernie. I know you can. Look at all the things you're doing now that you thought you couldn't do. Using the cell phone, paying your bills online. Arranging to get the RV fixed. You're a lot more capable than you think you are."

Ernestine picked up the bag of baby clothes, sat back down, and began smoothing the little shirts, the onesies, the soft blue sleepers, and blankets across her lap. "I know he won't give up driving. He just won't. We need to talk about something else."

"Okay," Clover said. "What?"

"Your mom. Tell me about her. You said you don't know if she'll let you stay."

"Well I don't know. But I'm hoping." Clover twisted a strand of hair. "She pretty much has to take me in, doesn't she? And maybe it'll be like you said. Maybe she'll be happy to have a grandbaby."

"I'm sure she will be," Ernestine said.

Clover got up to waddle to the bathroom. "I think the baby's stomping on my bladder. I have to pee every ten minutes."

Ernestine chuckled. "Well, he might not be stomping, but he's putting pressure on it for sure."

When Clover came out of the bathroom, Ernestine changed the subject. "How are you at cutting hair?" she asked.

"Pretty good, I think. Why?"

"Well, mine's getting shaggy. Do you think you could cut it for me?"

"Sure. I guess. Would you like me to dye it too? Your color's, like, really faded."

"It is, isn't it? That was the first dye job I ever had. My hairdresser talked me into it. Not sure I liked it."

"Why not? It looked good."

"Well, it's not really me."

"You could try a different color."

"Maybe..."

They left Walter sleeping and walked down the block to a drugstore. "I'm not sure this is a good idea,"

Ernestine said while they studied the Revlon boxes. "I don't think Walter will like it."

"You should do what you like."

"You're right, I guess. Coloring it did make me feel good."

When they got back to the motel, Ernestine realized the only scissors she had were the ones in her travel sewing kit. "They're not for cutting hair, but they'll have to do."

Clover draped a towel around Ernestine's shoulders. "How much should I take off?"

"I don't know. I like it pretty short."

"Okay, let's do it."

When she finished cutting, Clover put on the plastic gloves that came with the hair dye kit and worked the goop into Ernestine's hair with her fingers. Then she set a timer for thirty minutes.

By the time Walter woke up from his nap, Ernestine's hair was sticking straight up in stiff purple spikes. "Yikes," he said, "what happened to you?"

"Clover colored my hair. Do you like it?"

When he didn't answer, Ernestine turned to study herself in the mirror. "I'm not sure I like it either, but thank God I won't be seeing anybody I know."

29

It was 8:00 a.m. on the Monday after Ernestine's inquiry, when Daryl from the repair shop called.

"Mrs. Emmons, we have your RV ready. I'm sorry it took us so long to get all the parts, but it's finished."

"Oh, thank goodness," she said. "How does it look?"

"Like a brand new rig."

"We'll be over to get it as soon as my husband wakes up. Do I pay the deductible to you?"

"Yes, ma'am. Three thousand dollars. Insurance agreed to waive the deductible on that window incident."

It had been a chore walking Walter through the phone call to transfer forty-five hundred dollars from his mutual funds to their checking account. She'd had to coach him about the name and location of their bank, remind him of his own Social Security number, and repeat how much they needed. It was like he'd never dealt with money before. Now, it turned out they'd liquidated more than necessary. Better too much than not enough, she thought, who knows what else will come up?

She woke Walter. "The motorhome is ready. We can go pick it up."

"What motorhome?" She looked at him and felt like crying. Could he not remember anything? She wanted so badly to believe his confusion was temporary. But if he couldn't remember they had a motorhome, or where it was, how could she expect him to drive it? Disheartened, she sat on the edge of the bed. What were they going to do if he couldn't?

Walter sat up and scratched his head. "Did we have breakfast?"

"Not yet," she said. "I guess we should go do that."

While they ate, she watched him carefully, wondering what her next step should be. Of course her first priority was taking care of him, but she'd made a promise to a wayward pregnant girl, and she intended to keep it. Come hell or high water, she was going to get Clover home to Kansas. Right now, though, they had to return the Hummer and pick up the motorhome.

Walter polished off a stack of waffles and began talking about hitting the deer, the broken headlight, and getting back on the road now that the RV was fixed.

Intensely relieved, Ernestine grabbed onto low blood sugar as the likely cause of his confusion and told herself he'd be fine as long as she made sure he ate more often.

"Let's go get it," she said, handing him the key to the Hummer.

"Ernie, are you sure?" Clover asked.

"He's fine."

"But—"

"He's fine. You stay here with Yosie and Chip. We'll be back shortly."

All the way to the repair shop, Ernestine scrutinized Walter's driving, willing him to do everything right. He took a corner faster than she thought safe and nearly ran a red light, but she told herself those were minor things.

In the repair shop office, she wrote one check for the three-thousand dollar deductible on the motorhome repair and another one for five-hundred eighty dollars to cover the damage to the Hummer where it had scraped the canyon wall. With that taken care of, Daryl shepherded them to the back of the lot where the Allegro was parked.

"It looks good," Ernestine said. "Don't you think so, Walter?"

"Whose is it?"

Her stomach clenched. "It's ours."

"No, it isn't."

Daryl raised his eyebrows. "Ma'am? Which one of you is driving?" He sounded concerned.

With Clover's warning about lawsuits ringing in her ears, Ernestine held out her hand for the key. "I am."

Walter climbed in and Ernestine, right behind him, guided him into the passenger seat. Once he was buckled in, she slid behind the steering wheel. The cab felt larger from this side. She adjusted the seat, moving it forward and up so she could reach the pedals. The windshield, bigger than the picture window in her house, was so close to her face she felt she would tip nose-first onto the pavement. Daryl stood watching. She wished he would go away. To kill time, she arranged the mirrors, checked the gauges, fiddled with things in the glove box, and pretended to look at her atlas. Finally, when she couldn't delay any longer, she put the motorhome in gear and stepped on the gas. It didn't move. She looked down. The emergency brake was on. She released it and tried again. With a burning face, a racing heart, and Daryl still watching, she made it to the edge of the lot where she caught the curb with her rear wheel and bumped onto the street.

Inching her way to the intersection, a red light allowed her a couple of minutes to breathe, to try to calm the fluttering in her gut. The light changed and she crawled forward, but not before someone behind her honked their horn. "Okay, okay, I'm going." She went two more blocks without having to stop at a light and talked herself all the way back to the motel. "Left turn at the next intersection. Get in the turn lane. Green arrow. Good. Three more blocks. Motel is on the left." She pulled in, this time hitting a curb with the right front wheel, and stopped so abruptly that Walter's seat belt practically choked him. She sat still, willing her heart to slow and her hands to stop shaking.

Walter, who'd ridden the whole way without saying a word, freed himself from the belt, stood up, and looked around. "Is this ours?"

"How does the motorhome look?" Clover asked when they got back to the room.

Without answering, Ernestine dropped her pocketbook and flopped face-down on the bed.

"You all right?" Clover asked.

"I just scared myself half to death."

"What do you mean?"

"I mean, driving that thing is scary."

"You drove it? Good for you. I mean not good that you, like, scared yourself. But good that you drove it."

"I was a nervous wreck."

"But you did it, didn't you? And now you know you can. It's just like driving a car, right?"

"Not quite," Ernestine said sitting up. "Can we just stay here one more day? I need time to recover before I have to drive that damn thing again."

30

"I had the strangest dream," Ernestine told Clover the next morning. "I was driving the motorhome and we were in a city somewhere in heavy traffic. There was a big truck riding my bumper and I kept trying to get him to back off. I slowed way down and he didn't pass. So I sped up, and he sped up. I went faster and faster and he stayed with me. I kept looking in the rearview mirror and he was so close I could see his face. It went on and on, and then finally he went around me, blowing his horn. I stuck my arm out the window and flipped him off."

Clover laughed.

"And you were with me. And Chip. You were holding a little boy, maybe two or three years old. Chip was big too. What do you think it means?"

"I think it means you're going to be one heck of a good driver."

Walter woke up hungry. "There's breakfast downstairs," Ernestine reminded him. "Let's eat before we take off."

They went down to the breakfast room where they'd eaten every morning for three weeks. "I like this place," he said. "Have we been here before?"

After they ate, Ernestine, having packed up everything the night before, waited with Walter in the RV while Clover went to get the pets. Nervous and surprised at Walter's lack of resistance to sitting in the swivel chair behind the cab, Ernestine settled herself behind the wheel.

When Clover arrived with the pets, Chip jumped on Walter, the two of them greeting each other so enthusiastically one would have thought they'd been separated for weeks.

"Come on," Walter said when the pup had calmed down and stretched out on the floor, "aren't we going to go?"

Ernestine took her time getting settled, trying to dispel the heart-pounding panic of the dream that was still with her. She felt unprepared to drive even a little ways, let alone the thousand miles to Manhattan, Kansas. Gripping the steering wheel, she closed her eyes and started to take deep breaths, holding each one before slowly letting it out.

"What are you doing?" Walter asked.

"This is supposed to help me relax. I saw it on TV." Having been interrupted, she started over and took several breaths, willing her heart rate to slow.

"Let's go, already."

Clover reached from the shotgun seat and patted Ernestine's arm. "You'll do fine. Just think about flipping off that truck driver."

Ernestine turned the key, and the engine rumbled to life. "Okay," she said, releasing her breath and the brake at the same time, "I'm as ready as I'll ever be. Which way?"

"Take a right." Clover said looking at the map on the iPhone. "We can stay on Route 66 toward Gallup, New Mexico. There's a KOA there. It's, like, a hundred eighty miles. That's probably far enough for your first day."

Ernestine pressed the gas pedal. Not feeling much response, she pressed harder sending Yosie and Chip sliding backward on the slippery vinyl. Picking up speed, she merged onto the highway, stayed in the right lane, and let cars zip by her. "Whew," she said, "here we go."

After a reasonable time for Ernestine to get comfortable driving, Clover turned toward the back. "Everybody looks cozy," she said. "Walter's on the sofa, Chip is curled up next to him, and Yosie's asleep on the bed. Do you mind if I turn on the radio?"

"No, of course not."

Clover fiddled with the knob. "What kind of music do you like?"

"I don't know, pretty much anything." It had been a long time since she'd given any thought to her taste in music. They rarely played any at home because Walter always had the TV on. He liked to watch old World War II movies and football games.

Coming across "Lean on Me," Clover took her hand off the knob. "How's this?"

"Perfect," Ernestine said, "I used to love that song."

"Who is that?"

"Bill somebody...Winters, Waters... can't remember for sure."

The song ended and the announcer broke in..."Bill Withers here on your Golden Oldies station. We'll be right back after this from one of our sponsors."

While the commercial droned on, Clover talked about her dad's record collection. "He had tons of vinyl albums. LPs, he called them. Like, that's so funny, we just stream our music now."

"Stream?"

"Yeah, like, we download it from the internet."

"Oh dear," Ernestine said, "I am so out of touch with things." She turned her attention to the radio and as the songs played, one after another, she was surprised to realize she actually knew most of the lyrics. As she sang along, memories flooded her senses. Memories of how handsome Walter was. And how romantic. She remembered their first date, and how well they danced together. When the voices of Simon and Garfunkel singing "Bridge Over Troubled Waters" filled the cab, she said, "It's been ages since I heard that song. It was one of our favorites, Walter's and mine. We used to compete in dance contests. Can you picture that? We even won a few times."

Clover grinned. "Sure, I can. I'll bet you were good."

Still humming, Ernestine checked the rearview mirror and passed a slow moving truck. "You were right, you know. Driving this really isn't all that different from driving a car. I was just so scared to try. How am I doing?"

"You're doing awesome."

"You can change the station if you want. Find something you like."

"You sure?"

"Yes," Ernestine said, "and thanks for turning it on. That music brought back some wonderful memories."

Clover turned the dial, and landed on some loud, distorted guitar sounds. Ernestine made a face. "Is that what you kids listen to?"

"In California we did. Pretty rad, huh?"

"I'm not sure what rad is, but it's pretty awful."

Clover leaned in and twisted the dial again. "At home in Kansas, we always listened to country."

"Why don't you find some of that?"

So for miles, they listened to Garth Brooks, Kenny Chesney, Faith Hill, and the like, and watched truck after truck after truck come from the opposite direction. It was a long time before either of them spoke again.

"Where are they all coming from?" Ernestine wondered. "And what are they carrying?"

A ways farther on, she spied a Flying J Truck Stop and pulled in. "Let's get out and move around. I need a break and so does Walter. He's been sleeping way too much."

Inside the store, she helped Walter find the Men's room before going into the Ladies'. Even though she was used to the tiny bathroom in the RV, she took advantage of larger restrooms every time she could. It felt almost luxurious having all that space. She jumped when she passed the mirrors, then chuckled. She looked different, and it wasn't just her hair that surprised her. There was something else. A boldness, or what her mother used to call pluck. She'd been driving the motorhome for more than fifty miles, something she thought she'd never do, and she was proud of herself. She freshened her lipstick and came out of the restroom to find Walter standing by the coffee dispensers looking lost.

"Here I am, Dear," she said taking his hand. "Do you want to get something to eat? They've got a deli, and Krispy Kreme donuts."

She wasn't surprised when he said, "Donuts." He'd always been into sweets. She picked out some crullers and a couple of maple bars, handed the bag to him, and filled two cups with coffee. Then meeting Clover at the cash register, she suggested they sit down where there were tables by the window.

While they were eating, an old man, maybe Walter's age, wandered in from outside. Ernestine noticed the panicky look in his eyes as he stood first by the coffee counter, then by the door of the ladies room, and then shuffled back toward where he'd come in.

"I wonder if he's looking for his wife." Ernestine kept watching him as he wandered outside, put his hands and face against the window glass and gazed in. "Someone should help him." She started to get up, and then noticed that a younger man had joined him.

Clover touched Ernestine's shoulder. "I bet that's his son. They look alike don't they?"

Ernestine sat back down but continued to watch. The younger man took the old man's arm and led him to a red pickup truck with an Arkansas license plate that was loaded with furniture tied down with ropes.

Back on the road, Ernestine couldn't shake the image of that old man.

31

Even though Ernestine still held some resentment over Walmart's effect on small businesses like Walter's, she found them to be convenient. So when she spotted one in Winslow, Arizona, she pulled off the highway and parked the motorhome toward the back of the lot.

"We've run out of some things," she said to Walter, "do you want to come in the store with us?"

"No," he said, scratching Chip's ears. "I'll stay here with my buddy."

"Okay." She pointed at the entrance. "We'll be right in there. We won't be long."

She was in the meat department, trying to decide if she wanted ground beef or chicken, when she heard over the loudspeaker: "Will the family of the elderly gentleman named Walter please come to the customer service desk?"

"Oh shit," she said handing the shopping list to Clover. "You finish. I need to go get him."

When Walter saw Ernestine, he broke away from the tall, dark-haired woman whose arm was draped protectively around his shoulders. The look in his eyes was the same panicky expression she'd seen on the old man at the truck stop.

"I didn't know where you went," he said. "I couldn't find you."

The woman glared at Ernestine. "He was wandering in the parking lot. He said you left him and didn't say where you were going."

Bristling at the implied accusation, Ernestine took Walter's hand. "Of course I told him where I was going. I'll take over now, thank you."

"You know," the woman sniffed, "you shouldn't leave him alone."

People were gawking and Ernestine fought to retain her composure. Not only was it frightening that Walter was wandering around in the parking lot, but it was humiliating as well. She gave Walter's hand a slight tug, and feeling resistance, let go and hung back letting him walk in front of her. Suddenly she was hit with a cascade of gut wrenching realizations. Walter was going down the same rabbit hole as Clover's grandpa and that old man they saw at the Flying J. His memory lapses weren't due to his age, or being tired, or having low blood sugar, or any of the things she told herself because she didn't want to accept the truth.

Ernestine stood in a puddle of self-pity. Like two signposts pointing in opposite directions, the choice of whether to turn around and go home or continue on to Kansas stopped her in her tracks. She'd promised to take Clover to Kansas, and Walter, who for forty-two years had been her strength and support, her companion, her lover, was falling apart before her eyes. As reluctant as she'd been to accept what was happening, she couldn't deny the changes in him or the loneliness she felt. It was like being on a two-man raft with a person who forgot how to paddle. It made her sad. It made her scared. And it made her angry.

When they got to the grocery department where Clover was waiting with the shopping cart, Walter held out his arms. "Linda," he said, "I couldn't find you. I didn't know where you went."

"Well, here I am," Clover said ignoring that he'd called her Linda. "You found me. So we're good now."

As they moved slowly toward the checkout line, Clover whispered, "Do you think he'd wear a bracelet?"

"A bracelet?"

"Yeah. Dad got one for my grandpa. They're called MedAlert or something. They, like, engrave it with your names and a phone number. That way if he wanders off and gets lost, they know who to call."

"Do you know where I can get one?"

"I think Dad got it at a drugstore. You could ask at the pharmacy here."

While Clover took Walter and the shopping basket back to the motorhome, Ernestine headed to the pharmacy. They did have the bracelets and were able to do the engraving right there. Ernestine filled out the paperwork and, in less than fifteen minutes, left with what she thought was a rather handsome piece of jewelry.

Back in the RV she handed it to Clover, who fastened it on Walter's wrist, saying, "Hey, Walter, that looks really good on you."

"What's this? Get it off," he said, trying to undo the clasp.

"Leave it alone, Walter." Ernestine said. "It's so we can find you if you get lost again."

"I didn't get lost. I was looking for you."

Clover lifted Walter's arm and admired the bracelet.

"I think it looks really sexy. Don't you think so, Ernie?"

Walter looked at his wife and winked. "Is that right?"

Still reeling with the realization of what was happening, Ernestine took his free hand in hers. "Absolutely," she said. "Sexy as hell."

32

The scorn in that woman's eyes had left Ernestine feeling bitter, and that bitterness sapped her strength. "I can't face a long drive tonight," she told Clover. "Can we find something closer than Gallup?"

She had briefly framed her dilemma as a choice between heading home and continuing on to Kansas, but in fact she'd already decided. She didn't know how fast Walter's condition would escalate, but she had a pretty good idea about Clover's, and she fully intended to get her home.

"There's a couple places in Holbrook." Clover said looking up from the guide book. "We can try one of them."

It was still daylight when they pulled into the Petrified Forest KOA in Holbrook, and Walter got out of the rig to begin the setup. Ernestine watched in amazement while he leveled the rig, hooked up the electricity and sewer, and opened the slide outs as efficiently as ever. The paradoxes were baffling. How was it that he could remember how to do this, and not remember that she was in Walmart?

By the time the setup was finished it had gotten dark. Clover went off to the bathhouse and Ernestine turned on the interior lights and started to make dinner. Walter went to the bedroom in the back of the rig and began opening and closing closet doors.

"What are you looking for?" Ernestine called.

"My fishing pole. Where is it?"

"I think you put it in the storage area underneath."

"I need it."

"Now?"

"I need it."

"We'll get it in the morning. You can't go fishing now. It's dark."

"I need my fishing pole!"

"But why now? It's dark. Let's look for it tomorrow."

"I want it. Where is it?" He was pacing from the bedroom to the tiny kitchen, back and forth, opening every cabinet door, and getting in Ernestine's way.

"For crying out loud, Walter, you have to sit down. I'm trying to cook." He kept pacing back and forth.

"Walter, please. You're in my way."

Back and forth. Back and forth.

"Walter, SIT DOWN!" She hadn't meant to yell.

When Clover returned from the bathhouse, Ernestine and Walter were sitting at the table drinking wine and the makings of dinner were still on the kitchen counter.

"I don't know if the wine was a good idea or not," Ernestine said, "but he got anxious and I couldn't think of any other way to calm him down. I was making tacos. Would you mind finishing up? You know how to do that don't you?"

By the time the tacos were ready, Walter was well into his third glass of wine and not interested in eating. Ernestine's plan to calm him had worked so well that she and Clover had to walk him to the bed and undress him.

Ernestine sat up long after he and Clover were sleeping, thinking through the whole evening. The pacing wasn't entirely new, but it had never been this bad. She hadn't meant to yell at him, and having done that, she gave him wine.

Never heavy drinkers, they'd occasionally unwound with a few glasses of wine, but the amount he'd had tonight unwound him so well he was practically under the table.

Pathetic as it was the thought of him being "under the table" caused her to chuckle. One New Year's Eve in particular stood out in her memory. They'd gone dancing but got home before midnight. Walter built a fire in the fireplace and they turned on the TV to watch the Ball drop in New York City. Even though they'd had a lot of wine already, the unopened bottle of champagne they'd bought for the occasion was too tempting to leave alone. Ernestine had always believed Linda was conceived that night. Suddenly, it struck her how much she missed that intimacy. How long had it been?

Months? Years? Aglow with the memory, she crawled into bed and pressed her body against Walter's back. She ran her hand along his side and down his hip, curled her toes into the bottoms of his feet, and fell asleep.

33

As they approached Gallup, New Mexico, Ernestine started seeing billboards for trading posts that sold, among other things, Navaho rugs, and was reminded of a friend who collected them. She'd always admired those rugs and wished for one of her own.

Other than the billboards, there wasn't much of interest. Buildings were few and far between, and most of those were rundown mobile homes. She'd seen movies where people lived in places like this, and imagined how hard their lives must be.

When they got to Gallup in the late afternoon, it was hot and dusty, and some sort of Native American festival was going on. The main street was blocked off and the sides were lined with spectators and artisans' stalls. People in feathers and war paint shook rattles and danced in the street to the beat of drums. This time it was Walter who said, "Let's get out and walk around before we go to the campground." Nervous about the rutted roads, Ernestine eased onto a side street and parked beside what looked like an abandoned gas station. Walter headed out the door, followed by Ernestine, Clover, and the dog.

Taking a leisurely pace, the three of them stopped every once in a while to watch the dancers. They made it to a plaza, where dozens of tent awnings were set up over displays of jewelry, clay pots, and all sorts of hand-crafted items. Ernestine, happy to indulge herself in something cultural, kept stopping to admire what the vendors were selling. Then she spotted the tables stacked with Navaho rugs. She had admired them from a distance so many times, but she'd never experienced the feel of them, or been in a position to appreciate the workmanship.

"Look at these, Walter," she said more than once, while rubbing a hand over the densely woven textiles. "Feel it. Look at these intricate designs."

Walter didn't share Ernestine's enthusiasm, so Clover took his arm and led him toward a display of wood carvings. Ernestine wandered on, making her way through the stacks, picking up one rug after anoher. They varied in price from a few hundred to several thousand dollars.

Ever since Clover showed Ernestine how to check her credit card balance, she'd done it almost obsessively, anticipating a huge charge from the Las Vegas casino to appear. But so far, the only amounts to show up were for the room and the breakfast she'd been too upset to finish. Unless gambling charges took longer to process, it was becoming clear that she hadn't used her credit card in the casino after all.

As she saw it, not having over-spent in Vegas gave her permission to do so now. She'd always wanted a Navaho rug, and this might be her only chance to get one. Looking around to see if Walter was nearby, she settled on a three by five foot rug with a red, black, and grey repeated diamond design, and handed the merchant her credit card. Then with her purchase wrapped in brown paper, she located Walter and Clover in the crowd.

"What's that?" Walter asked.

"I bought myself a little present."

He didn't ask to see it, so she didn't show him, and instead of feeling guilty, she felt proud of herself. She'd done something she'd never dared do before. She'd spent a thousand dollars without even discussing it with him.

Buying that rug was a turning point for Ernestine. As devastating as Walter's situation was, she was gaining a sense of her own authority. Always before, he had made the money decisions, and being beyond frugal, never wanted to touch a penny of their savings. They'd taken no vacations and never indulged in anything he considered unnecessary, which was why she was so surprised when he decided to buy the motorhome. She wasn't bitter about it, but she couldn't help wishing they'd gotten the motorhome when Linda was young. Wishing they'd taken a trip like this when she and Walter were stronger, before he'd gotten so forgetful.

So, she reasoned, buying something she wanted...well it wasn't just extravagance, it was liberation.

Feeling a bit giddy, Ernestine drove into the assigned space in the Gallup KOA, aligned the Allegro with the power pole, parked, and mentally patted herself on the back. Walter reached for the door handle.

"I'll get us hooked up." He took one step down, and fell. His left hip hit the ground hard. Ernestine hurried to his side. "Are you hurt?"

"I don't know."

"Can you get up?"

He waved her away.

"Do you want to try?"

"Leave me here. I'll get up in a minute."

She and Clover stood over him and waited. The ground was cold and gravelly, and he looked helpless lying there. After a few minutes, Ernestine prodded, "Now?"

When he nodded, she took one arm, Clover took the other, and they stood him up. Once they had him back inside, he alternated between holding his hip and limping, and insisting he was fine. The more he denied pain, the more pronounced his limp became. Ernestine suggesting an ice-pack triggered an argument that escalated until Clover stepped in.

"I took a first aid class in school," she said as she eased him into the swivel chair. "And they, like, said to elevate." She bent down, lifted his left foot, and placed it on the bench that surrounded the dinette. "And they said to ice the affected area." When Walter didn't protest, she took the ice-pack from Ernestine and placed it between his hip and the arm of the chair.

"You sit there and rest," Ernestine said. "Clover and I will take care of the setup." Outside, she told Clover, "I never had him show me how to do this."

"But he showed me."

Ernestine watched as Clover demonstrated what hooked up to where, how to run the leveling jacks, where the controls were for the slide-outs, and once they were done, Clover said, "See, now there's another thing you know how to do."

Just then Ernestine noticed a short, round woman with a distinctive walk coming toward them. Gladys Godfrey! What the hell was she doing here? Ernestine had hoped beyond hope that they wouldn't run into anyone they knew and her bizarre hair color was only part of it. If word got back to Linda about Walter's weakened condition, she'd insist they go home. And how on earth was she going to explain the girl?

"As I live and breathe," Gladys panted coming up to her. "If it isn't Ernestine Emmons."

"Gladys. My goodness. What are you doing here? I didn't know you had an RV."

Gladys sidled up to Ernestine and squinted at her. "What in blazes have you done to your hair?"

Ernestine touched her head. "Oh, I think it's fun. Do you like it?"

"Well *I* certainly wouldn't do it," Gladys scoffed. She turned her gaze to Clover. "Who's this?"

Ernestine searched for a plausible explanation—one that wouldn't seem too odd. To buy time, she asked, "Where's your rig?"

Gladys pointed over her shoulder, "Right over there by the bathhouse." She repeated her question. "So who is this ... very pregnant young woman?"

Ernestine turned toward where Gladys pointed. "That fifth-wheel? We looked at one of those before we bought this. How do you like it?"

"We like it *fine*. Who's the girl?"

"Oh, she's my niece."

"Your niece? Your brother's girl? I thought he had all boys."

"His wife's girl. Former marriage."

Gladys looked dubious, as though trying to recall what she knew about Ernestine's brother and his wife. She turned to Clover and reached to pat her belly. "It looks like you're about to deliver that little miracle." Clover stepped back.

"So where is Walter? Off somewhere? Leaving the work to you two? Do you want me to send George over to help?"

"No, no. We're done here."

"Are you sure? You know my George. Always ready to help where he can."

"No thank you. We've got it." Ernestine put her foot on the retractable step and opened the motorhome door. "Excuse us. We need to get supper started. Good to see you, Gladys."

When Clover stepped in behind her, Ernestine shut the door and leaned against it. "Shit!"

"Who was that?"

"A busybody from my church."

"You don't like her?"

Ernestine rolled her eyes. "I didn't expect to see anybody from home."

"Why did you say I was your niece?"

"I don't know. I couldn't think of anything else."

"Why couldn't you just say..."

"That we picked up a hitchhiker?"

"Yeah."

"Because word might get back to our daughter."

"Why does that matter?"

"Because you're pregnant … and she … well I'd just rather she didn't know." Ernestine opened the refrigerator and closed it again.

"Does she have something against pregnant girls that aren't married, is that it?"

"No. She doesn't. But I did."

"Huh? It doesn't seem like… I mean, why did you..."

"Why did I pick you up? I'm not sure. Maybe because you needed help. Maybe to make amends."

"I don't get it. Amends for what?"

"Well, honey, it's complicated. Like you, my daughter ran off when she was seventeen. She was gone for four months. We didn't know where she was. If she was alive or dead. And when she came home, she was pregnant."

"Oh. And you were...what?"

"Furious. I said some awful things to her." Not wanting Clover to see the tears the memory evoked, Ernestine turned her back and pulled a package of ground beef from the refrigerator.

Clover waited.

When Ernestine spoke again, her voice was thick. "I told her she'd shamed us. Said her father and I wouldn't be able to hold our heads up in town. And worse." She stopped talking, sniffed a few times, and started working with the hamburger, shaping it into patties.

Smelling the meat, Chip jumped off Walter's lap and wrapped himself around Ernestine's legs. She tried to push him away, but he stayed by her ankles and whined. Wiping her eyes with the back of her hand, she tossed him a hunk of hamburger which he caught in mid-air.

"I don't think he even tasted it," Clover said.

Chip begged for more but Ernestine, ignoring him, put the patties in a frying pan and flipped on the overhead fan.

"So, Ernie, what happened?" Clover prodded. "You made up didn't you? I mean you, like, talk and stuff."

"Ernestine reached for a tissue and blew her nose. "Yes, we talk. But she's never forgotten what I said."

"Did she keep the baby?"

"Oh yes, she kept the baby. It all worked out. She and Matt got married. They have two boys now, Jack and Jeremy, not much younger than you."

"So why can't you tell her about me?"

"I will. I just want to wait until I get you home."

213

Ernestine washed her hands and looked out the window toward the Godfrey's fifth-wheel. Her resistance to have Linda know wasn't about the girl being pregnant; it was about taking her all the way to Kansas. She was certain Linda wouldn't approve, and she just didn't feel like taking on the fight.

"I was rude just now, wasn't I?"

"No! But she was! How dare she say that about your hair? She was, like, aren't you going to ask me in?"

"I know. I suppose I should have."

"Why? She was being bitch."

Startled at first by Clover's remark, Ernestine shrugged and thought she's right. Gladys is a bitch.

Clover left to check on Walter who was dozing in the chair. Ernestine watched her touch him gently on the shoulder, speak softly to him, and reposition his ice pack, and she realized once again how much she would miss Clover when she was gone.

"Tell me about Linda," Clover said while she set out plates for dinner. "Like when she was younger. Did you get along?"

"We did when she was little. I didn't go back to work after she was born, so I was always home with her. She was my whole life. We had good times together. I loved to sew and I made her lots of pretty, frilly dresses, Halloween costumes, that sort of thing."

"I wish my mom had done that."

"After she started school, though, she stopped liking it. Said the clothes I made were ugly and embarrassing. She didn't like any of the store-bought clothes I picked out for her either."

"Didn't you let her pick out her own clothes?"

"Well, yes, eventually. Then she started gaining weight and nothing looked good on her and that was my fault too."

"It bothered you that she was heavy?"

"Yes it bothered me. I tried restricting what she ate. Thought I was helping, but it seemed to make matters worse between us. We fought a lot. She was never happy with anything I did. I was too old-fashioned, too strict."

Clover watched Ernestine put a generous scoop of mayonnaise into the potato salad she was making.

"Walter said I was making too much of it. Said I should leave her alone and let her figure it out on her own."

"And?"

"And I just couldn't. I hated seeing her bulk up the way she was."

"Was that the only thing you fought about?"

Ernestine put the salad on the table and sat down across from Clover.

"Unfortunately, no. She got mixed up with a bad crowd. Kids who drank and smoked marijuana. She swore she didn't do either of those things. That she just liked hanging out with them because they were fun. But then we found a stash of pot in her room. Walter grounded her for a month. And somehow, even that was my fault."

"Did she smoke pot again?"

"I don't know. I'm not even sure she ever did. But Walter and I were dead set against it, and since she had lied to us about other things, we didn't believe her about that."

"Wow," Clover said.

"It wasn't long after that, when she ran off."

"With Matt?"

"Yeah. With Matt. And she came home pregnant."

"Is she still fat?"

Ernestine chuckled. "No. After she had the boys, she slimmed way down. She looks terrific now."

"Well, I wish you didn't have to lie about who I am. I mean, I never, like, wanted to cause trouble with your family."

All evening, Walter sat with his leg elevated, claiming first that his hip hurt and then that it didn't. When Ernestine offered Tylenol, he shoved it away. He complained, swore, denied any pain, swore, and complained again. After convincing him to go to bed, Ernestine poured herself a large glass of wine and collapsed on the sofa. "I need this," she said to Clover, "maybe it will help me unwind."

When Ernestine started on a second glass, Clover said, "Hey, do you have any games?"

"Look in the cabinet under the TV."

Clover dug around in the cabinet. "Wow," she said, "you have lots of games in here. I haven't seen you guys playing any of 'em."

"I know. I thought we would. We used to play all the time."

"Why don't you now?"

"We tried a few times, but he got frustrated, so we quit."

Clover pulled out the Checkers. "Do you mind if we play?"

"I'd like that."

As soon as Clover unfolded the board and spilled the checkers onto the table, Yosie jumped up and batted at the disks, sending them skidding everywhere.

"Bad kitty," Clover said. She set the kitten on the floor and got on her knees to reach under the table and sofa for the scattered pieces.

Ernestine couldn't help but laugh at how awkward she looked crawling on the floor. "Come on," she chuckled, "get up. Let me get them with the broom." When the pieces were back on the table and Yosie was winding up to spring again, Ernestine picked her up and relocated her to the bathroom.

"I used to, like, beat my dad at checkers all the time," Clover said, making the first move. "I think he let me win though."

"Do you miss him?"

"My dad? Yeah, I do. I miss the way he used to be. Before Bonnie. He changed a lot after she came."

"Hmmm, that's too bad," Ernestine said, jumping one of Clover's checker pieces and claiming it. "Wouldn't it be nice if we could make people the way they used to be?"

"Yeah. You're thinking about Walter aren't you?"

"I suppose I am. He was always so smart. So good at games. Good at everything."

Clover took her turn and hopped over three of Ernestine's pieces.

"Oops." Ernestine took a sip of wine. "Looks like I don't remember how to play either."

"You're just distracted.   Mind if I ask you a question?"

"Of course not."

"What're you going to do when you get home?"

"What do you mean?"

"About Walter. Will you have any help?"

Ernestine fiddled with the checker pieces in front of her, stacking them, taking them apart, and stacking them again.

"What about Linda?" Clover pushed on. "Will she help?"

"I couldn't ask her to do that. Her boys are still young. She's needed at home."

Clover moved a checker. "Your turn."

Ernestine moved a piece and Clover moved a piece. They went back and forth until Clover, seeing an opportunity, jumped three in a row and ended the game. "I hope," she said, starting to gather up the pieces, "I didn't, like, say too much. I'm just worried about you."

34

By the following morning, an ugly bruise had developed on Walter's left hip and the limping was worse. "We need to have him x-rayed to see if anything's broken," Ernestine said. She started to go outside to begin the take-down process, saw Gladys beside the bathhouse, and changed her mind. Every few minutes she pulled the front curtains apart just enough to see out. When Gladys was no longer in sight, she nudged Clover. "The coast is clear."

They worked fast. Ernestine undoing the water and sewer hoses and Clover taking care of the electrical cord and the slide outs. On the way out of the park, they drove past Gladys and George, both of whom looked puzzled, if not annoyed. "Wave, Walter," Ernestine said, "maybe they'll just think we're in a hurry."

The medical clinic, right off Highway 40, had a wide lot. The Allegro took up two spaces, but Ernestine had no trouble parking. Because they'd walked in without an appointment, they sat in the waiting room for over an hour, with Walter asking every few minutes, "What's going on here?" And Ernestine's, "Waiting to see the doctor," grew more snappish each time she said it.

"Walter Emmons," a woman in scrubs called. Walter stood with a grunt. "Mrs. Emmons, do you want to come with him?"

When Ernestine grabbed her pocketbook, Walter stopped and turned back. "No." He pointed at Clover. "Her."

It stung, him wanting Clover instead of her, but she understood why. Clover was more relaxed with him than she was. "Go ahead, Clover, " she said, "he wants you, not me."

Ten minutes later Walter emerged from the x-ray room smiling. "I told you. Nothing's broken."

"They said to keep putting ice on it," Clover said. "And to get him a cane so he doesn't, like, fall again."

Red Rock Medical Supply, two doors down in the same strip mall, carried a large selection of canes, and Ernestine spent several minutes trying to decide which one to get. She suspected Walter would balk at using one of the lightweight metal ones with the cartoonish decorations and he'd be too vain to use a plain wood one like his father's. Then she spied a fancy **brass handled** model that claimed to be a replica of Bat Masterson's walking stick.

When she got back to the RV, Walter was settled with his leg elevated and the ice-pack on his hip. Ernestine handed him the cane. "Look what I found. Pretty classy, don't you think?"

"What the hell is that for?"

"It's for you, so you don't fall. The doctor said you should use one."

"Bullshit, I don't need that." He tossed it, and it skidded across the floor, scaring the puppy.

Discouraged, Ernestine picked it up and put it on the bed. It doesn't matter what I tell him, she thought, he's not going to listen to me. When she got settled in the driver's seat, Walter approached from the back and told her to move. "Let me drive," he said.

"No," she said, "I'm driving. You go sit down."

"I said get up."

"Walter, I want to drive."

"Look, I've been driving since I was fifteen years old."

"Yes, I know you have, and you're very good at it, but I need to drive because I need practice."

"Practice, why?"

What was it Clover had said to do instead of arguing? Flatter him.

"So I can be as good a driver as you."

"Oh," Walter said dropping into the passenger seat. "Go ahead then. I guess you do need practice."

Taking a deep breath, Ernestine put the RV in gear and headed toward Albuquerque.

"You know," Clover said from behind Walter where she was looking at the atlas, "Albuquerque is south of here. Shouldn't we be going north?"

"Uh, yes."

"I think we could, like, save time if we cut off at a place called Thoreau and take 371. It goes straight north to Farmington."

"Well, I guess that makes sense, doesn't it? Let's try that."

The sign at the junction said: THOREAU, POPULATION 1,863. Turning onto the highway, Ernestine noted the juniper trees, sagebrush, and tumbleweeds. At first, the two-lane road with its fifty-five-mile-an-hour speed limit was unchallenging. She stayed steady and let cars pass her. After a while, though, the road turned curvy and hilly, and she slowed to fifty, then forty-five. PASS WITH CARE signs appeared every few hundred yards, and in the rearview mirror, she saw a long line of cars behind her, zig-zagging back and forth, checking to see if it was safe to pass.

"Speed up," Walter said. "Speed up!"

When the big black pickup that had been tailgating her passed blowing its horn, Clover leaned forward and whispered, "Remember your dream." Ernestine stuck her arm out the window, middle finger up.

"Good for you," Clover laughed. "I knew you could do it."

Emboldened, Ernestine pushed down hard on the accelerator. When the needle hit 75 mph, Walter chuckled, "There you go, Ernie. There you go."

The officer who pulled her over was surly. Coming from the opposite direction, he'd seen her flip off the pickup driver and then speed up. First he chewed her out for going too fast, and when she tried to explain about the cars tailgating her when she went the speed limit, he lectured her about pulling over to let them go around.

"I could cite you for impeding traffic, too," he said, ripping the ticket from his book, shoving it in her direction, and then tipping his hat.

"Well that was damned unnerving," she said. "Just when I was getting the hang of driving this thing."

"Let me drive," Walter said. "I'll show that..."

"No, you won't," she snapped. On top of everything else, she didn't feel like arguing about who was going to drive.

"Clover, honey," she said, "Would you get me that hat I bought?"

"The one from Route 66?"

"Yes, and would you see if you can locate my sunglasses?"

Wearing the hat and sunglasses, she set the cruise control to fifty-five and got back on the highway. Whenever there were more than two cars behind her, she pulled over to the side and let them pass. Occasionally there was a cow or a herd of sheep crossing the road, but there wasn't much to see scenery-wise. Like other parts of the southwest, it was all scrub brush, junipers, and huge steep-sided rock formations.

It was after one o'clock when she found a place to pull off the road. She made sandwiches, and after they'd eaten, Walter, who had been sleeping on and off all morning, said he needed a nap. "It's all he does," she said, watching him stagger to the back where the bed was.

"Grandpa was like that," Clover said. "Slept most of the time. At night, though, sometimes he'd, like, get up and try to get out of the house, say he had to go to work."

"What kind of work did he do?"

"He worked at the university in Manhattan. He was a dean or something. Retired a long time ago. Before I was born even."

Ernestine stood and cleared away the lunch things. "We'd better get going. Why don't you come sit up front with me?"

As she drove, Ernestine's thoughts drifted to the challenges ahead of her. Once she got Clover to Manhattan, she had the whole drive home, by her calculations, almost twenty-five hundred miles. She couldn't let Walter drive, and now with his bad hip, he couldn't do anything physical. She'd have to locate the places to stay, do the set-ups and take-downs, the sewage disposal, everything. Just thinking about it made her tired. She'd already taken on so much. What would it be like once they got home? Would she need help? How would she go about finding someone? What would it cost?

Clover, sitting beside her, was engrossed in something on the iPhone when thunder boomed and rain started pounding the windshield. Suddenly Chip, panting and shaking, cowered between Ernestine and Clover, and when Clover reached down to pet him he jumped up onto what was left of her lap.

35

Cloudburst over, Clover pointed at a billboard. "Would it be okay if we stop and see that?"

"What? Bisti Badlands? What is it?"

"Google says it's like a fantasy world of strange rock formations. Can we?"

"I don't see why not. We need a break anyway." Pulling off on a muddy road and trying to avoid puddles, Ernestine followed the arrows. When they were parked, Clover put Chip on his leash and lumbered down the steps. Ernestine followed, helping Walter navigate.

They found themselves in the midst of the weirdest landforms Ernestine had ever seen. Printed signs identified "hoodoos," "pinnacles," "spires," shapes so bizarre she couldn't imagine how they came up with the names.

"I wish we could, like, be here at sunset," Clover said, aiming the phone's camera. "I'll bet the colors are amazing." She took a few shots and then handed the phone to Ernestine. "You should be the one taking pictures. I'll take Chip for a walk."

"Stand over there first," Ernestine said. "And turn sideways. I want a picture of you before you have the baby."

Ernestine then took a few random shots of the landscape and a few more of Walter with the formations in the background.

"What is this place," he asked.

"It's called Bisti Badlands. We're in New Mexico."

"We were here once," Walter said.

"We were?"

"Yes, and we saw Mount Rushmore, too."

"Oh, you mean South Dakota?"

"Yes. Right here. We brought Linda."

They'd never been in New Mexico before. They hadn't been to South Dakota either and they'd never taken Linda on a trip anywhere. Searching for an something to say to him, Ernestine realized he must be remembering when his parents took him on a vacation. He was seven or eight. He was the child, not Linda.

"That was a fun trip wasn't it?" she said.

Walter smiled. "It's nice to see it again."

Pleased to have pacified him, she turned and noticed the large wet spot on the front of his trousers.

"Come, sweetheart," she said, "We've had an accident. Let's get you some dry pants."

"Let's see if we can find a campground in Farmington," Ernestine said when everyone was back inside and buckled in. She knew they should get farther before they stopped for the night, but getting a speeding ticket and having Walter wet himself were enough challenges for one day.

Clover spent a few minutes searching with the phone. "Here's one," she said. "A Mom & Pop RV Park. It has five stars and good reviews."

The campground owners lived on-site in a mobile home that had a vast model railroad lay-out with bridges, buildings, trees, everything one could imagine, stretching the entire length of their house. "Mom and Pop" were super nice, too, greeting Ernestine, Walter, and Clover as though they were long-time friends. Pop, bearded and wearing bibbed overalls and a flannel shirt, was a talker. As soon as Walter got out of the motorhome, surprising Ernestine by using his cane, Pop invited him to tour the railroad.

They were assigned a space number and given instructions about how to find it, but Walter seemed to be enjoying the railroad so much, Ernestine was reluctant to interrupt.

"Why doesn't he stay here and visit while you take care of things?" the apple-cheeked woman said to Ernestine. "We'll walk him over when you're done."

"She could tell, couldn't she?" Ernestine said to Clover as she drove to the space. "Some people have really big hearts."

36

Ernestine was cleaning up after dinner when the iPhone started vibrating. "It's Linda. Want me to answer it," Clover teased.

Ernestine wiped her hands on a towel and reached for the phone. "Hello, dear. How are you?"

"I'm fine, Mom. What's going on with you anyway?"

"What do you mean, what's going on? We're on a trip."

"Well, Uncle Richard made a strange comment to me on Facebook."

"Oh?"

"He said, 'I think your mom's losing it.'"

"What's that supposed to mean?"

"That's what I wanted to know. I called him, and you know what he told me? He said his wife got an email from that old bat, Gladys Godfrey, congratulating her on becoming a grandma."

Shit, Ernestine thought. She was afraid that would happen.

"The email said they ran into you and Dad in a KOA in New Mexico, and that there was a pregnant girl with you. You told her it was your niece. Your brother's daughter from a first marriage. Is that true, Mom?"

"No. Well, yes. I mean we were at the same campground. We were both so surprised."

"But, Mom is that true? The other part. The pregnant girl? Richard's wife wasn't married before, was she?"

Ernestine forced a chuckle. "No, no, Gladys misunderstood. She can't hear very well, you know."

"What did she misunderstand?"

"I said the girl was *Denise*. She was camped next to us. I don't know where the rest of that came from."

Linda was quiet.

"Are you still there?"

"I'm here," Linda said. "So you're all right? Nothing's going on?"

"Nothing is going on."

"Gladys told Uncle Richard you were acting odd."

"Oh, phooey. No odder than usual. So how are you and the boys? Everything good there?"

"Yeah, Mom. We're fine. One other thing. Gladys said your hair is purple. Is it?"

"Yes it is. I tried to redo the red and it came out funny."

"Leave your hair alone. You're not a teenager."

"Linda, it's my hair."

"Okay, it's your hair, but when are you coming home?"

"I can't say for sure. Just don't worry about us."

When the call ended, Ernestine laid the phone on the table and put her head in her hands. She wondered if she would go to hell for lying.

It was a terrible night. For one thing, Ernestine couldn't stop thinking about the lies she'd told, and the consequences of telling them. For another, Walter kept getting up and wandering out to the front of the rig. Once she caught him trying the door. She got him back to bed, but lay awake the rest of the night worrying about what would happen next.

She regretted having to break camp the next morning because of how warm and welcoming the park owners had been. And the way Walter had perked up when he saw that railroad. Maybe building model trains would have been a good hobby for him. She wished he'd chosen that instead of getting an RV.

Parking the rig next to the owners' mobile home, Ernestine went inside to pay. "Thank you so much for your kindness," she said, shaking the old man's hand. "I would like to stay longer, but we're in a hurry."

"Where are you headed?" the woman asked.

"To Kansas. Manhattan, Kansas. I'm trying to get the girl home to her mother before the baby comes."

"Have you given any thought to your route?" Pop asked. "North of here is pretty mountainous."

"Well, I thought Route 550. What would you recommend?"

"Your husband isn't driving, is he?"

"Oh, no. It'll be me."

Pop removed his glasses and stroked his whiskers. "I think you've got yourself into a bit of a pickle. Going north from here at this time of year is dangerous. If it was me, I'd turn around and head back to Albuquerque, then take I-25 to Denver."

"But that's backtracking. I don't have that much time."

"That's a pretty bad road you're thinking about. Beautiful scenery, but—"

"She's due anytime, and I—"

"I still think you'd be better off."

"Well, okay then." Ernestine shook his hand one more time. "Thanks again."

Ernestine considered doing what he said, but she'd been noticing how Clover walked with her hands on the small of her back, how often she was going to the bathroom, and how far the baby had dropped, and knew they couldn't risk an extra day.

Choosing to keep Pop's advice to herself, she opted for Route 550. By the time they got to Durango, Ernestine was so tense her whole body ached. From there north, Pop had said, it got really dangerous. Although the scenery was said to be spectacular, she couldn't afford to take her eyes off the road. The RV groaned its way up two ten-thousand-foot mountain passes where, on the left side the road dropped straight down with no guardrails, no shoulder, and nowhere to pull off. Ernestine crawled along, hugging the inside curves, getting so close in places that she scraped the side of the Allegro. Her body felt like an overstretched rubber band about to snap, and *Oh my God, Oh my God, Oh my God* played like an annoying song she couldn't get out of her head.

Before they reached the 11,018-foot Red Mountain Pass, it started to snow. Clover, who had been quiet for a long time, moved from the sofa, knelt behind Ernestine and dug her fingers into her shoulders. "You're really tight," she said. "Try to relax. Try to breathe. We're going to be okay."

"Isn't it kind of early for snow?" Ernestine's voice sounded thin from tension.

"It is almost the end of September," Clover said.

"I should have listened to that man at the campground."

"About what?"

"About coming this way. He said not to. Said it was too dangerous."

"You didn't tell me that. What did he suggest instead?"

"He said to go back down to Albuquerque and north from there. I was worried about losing time. You're going to have that baby any day, and I want to get you home before that happens."

Walter, in the front seat beside Ernestine, woke from his snooze, straightened up and opened his eyes. "A baby? We're having a baby?" He tried to stand, but the seatbelt held him down. "Let me hold her. Let me hold the baby." Seeing him flail around, Ernestine threw her right arm out, the way she used to do to protect Linda when she was a child. In doing so, she took her eyes off the road and went into a skid. The motorhome slammed into the rock wall and ground to a halt. For the longest time, they sat, motorhome snugged up to the snowy wall, while Ernestine cried out all the tension, fear, fatigue, frustration, and sadness she'd been holding in.

Several cars passed without stopping. Clover tried the phone but there was no service. "Even if nobody stops," she said, "someone will report seeing us here and send help. And at least we're, like, inside and warm." Almost as soon as she said that, a truck came by dispensing sand. "Pull out, Ernie," Clover said. "Quick. Follow him."

Slipping and sliding, Ernestine managed to get the Allegro back on the roadway. She followed the truck all the way to the junction with Highway 50, not caring about the grit that sprayed her windshield. Bellied up to the sand truck on the way down the mountain, she wrestled with her decision to keep things from Linda. The truck ramp, the bear in Yosemite, the collision with the deer, picking up Clover, and most importantly, Walter's decline. She considered calling, admitting she was afraid, and asking for help. She would explain about Clover and the promise she'd made, and even if Linda wasn't sympathetic, Matt might be.

At the junction, she pulled into a filling station and climbed out on legs of rubber. While the attendant pumped the gas, Ernestine walked around the side of the RV to see the damage. It wasn't as bad as when

Walter hit the wall at Linda's, but it was considerable. She went inside the convenience store that shared space with a McDonald's, paid for the gas, and bought herself a cup of coffee. Then she sat at one of the tables and called Linda.

"Hello, dear," she said when Linda picked up.

"Hi, Mom."

"It's snowing here..."

"Oh, where are you?"

"Colorado."

"Colorado? How much snow?"

"Not much." Ernestine took a deep breath and opened her mouth to say more, but the words wouldn't come.

"Mom?"

"I'm here. The snow is beautiful. Do you have snow?"

"Heavens no! It's in the high 80s here."

Although she'd planned to tell Linda everything, she lost her nerve. She'd gotten them off that mountain and the road was better now. She'd wait and call again after she got Clover home.

"Are you sure Dad's okay driving in it?"

"He's fine. I'll let you go. I just wanted to check in."

"Okay Mom... Mom?"

"What, dear?"

"I love you."

"I love you, too."

37

Before leaving the store, Ernestine asked the cashier how far it was to Glenwood Springs. He scratched his head, dropped his hand, and stared at his fingernails. "Depends. Over to Grand Junction, or you can trim off about fifty miles if you cut over at Delta and go up from there."

"How are the roads?"

"You done the worst of it," he said. "Should be pretty easy now." Ernestine thanked him and went back to the RV where Walter was limping back and forth, flapping his hands, and Clover was doing her best to calm him down.

"What is it? What's happening?" Ernestine asked

"He's just, like, really panicky. I told him you were coming right back, but he wouldn't stop pacing. Says you were gone too long." Clover stepped aside to allow Ernestine take over.

"I'm here, Sweetheart," Ernestine said. "I'm right here."

He kept pacing. Limping and pacing.

"Here, let's sit." She steered him to a chair. "I'm sorry I took so long, but I'm here now." He pulled away and paced some more.

They stayed parked in front of the store for over an hour while Ernestine, using the quietest, most reasonable voice she could summon, crooned and stroked Walter's forearms, until he began to relax.

Exhausted, she moved to the cab where Clover was already in the passenger seat.

"Ernie," Clover said, "you know marijuana is legal in Colorado, don't you?"

Ernestine looked at her sideways, "I think I read about that, why?"

"Well, I was, like, thinking we could get some for Walter."

"For Walter? No."

"I mean it. It could, like, help him chill. So he wouldn't get all anxious like he just did, and like he's been doing almost every evening. Lots of people are using it now. You know, like, for pain. And they say it helps with anxiety too."

"Really?"

"Yeah. There's, like, these studies." She fingered the iPhone. "I could show you..."

Ernestine waved the phone away. "No. Walter would never agree to that. No. Absolutely not."

"Okay," Clover shrugged her shoulders. "It was just a thought."

By the time Ernestine cut over at Delta, Clover's suggestion had wormed its way into her consciousness, masking the road's twists and curves. What if marijuana would help? What if Clover could talk Walter into it? Maybe if he knew it was legal he'd go along.

Brought up on the movie *Reefer Madness*, Ernestine had always heard that marijuana caused people to become addicted or commit heinous crimes or, at the very least, end up with brain damage. She also knew that those claims had since been disputed. But even if it was legal, marijuana carried an air of delinquency.

"Clover," she said after a while, "what you said about marijuana...do you think we could get some in Glenwood Springs?"

"Sure, but aren't you, like, too tired to drive that far?"

"Not anymore," Ernestine said. The prospect of doing something daring had revived her, leaving her almost giddy.

"Okay then," Clover grinned. "That's a plan."

Ernestine sped up and kept pace with the rest of the traffic, her confidence increasing as rapidly as the elevation. At the McClure Pass viewpoint, where several tour buses were parked, she decided to pull in.

Walter peered out the side window. "Where are we?"

"We're in Colorado."

"What are we doing here?"

"Well, right now we're going to get out and look at the scenery."

"Sounds good," Clover said. "I'll bring Chip."

Standing at the railing with Walter, Clover, and the dog, Ernestine was dumbfounded by the view. "I'm going to get the phone," she said to Clover. "You and Chip stand by Walter. I want to take your picture."

"Now let me get you two," Clover said, taking the phone from Ernestine. "Smile. Look like you're having a good time." Ernestine wondered if they were. She especially wondered if Walter was. It was hard to tell.

They were about to get back in the RV when a young man from one of the tour buses approached them. "Would you like me ... he pointed at the phone. "All of you in the picture."

"That would be great." Clover handed him the phone and herded Walter and Ernestine back to the railing. "Here," she said, boosting the dog into Walter's arms, you hold him." She stood on Walter's right side and Ernestine got on his left. The three of them put their heads together and smiled. After thanking the young man, Clover pressed the review button and showed Ernestine the picture. Behind them was a backdrop of blue snow-capped mountains, red rock cliffs, golden aspen trees, and Colorado's majestic fourteen-thousand-foot Maroon Bells. They all looked happy, especially Walter, who had the biggest, brightest smile he'd worn since the day Clover showed up with the puppy.

38

The RV Park in Glenwood Springs was on a side street and poorly lit, so Ernestine was eager to get settled before it got any darker. When she went into the office to register, the woman behind the counter took her money and asked if she had a dog. Ernestine said she did.

"Keep it on a leash and clean up after it," the woman snapped. "I'm sick of picking up after everyone's dogs."

Ernestine was attaching the RV's sewer hose when she heard retching on the other side of the rig. She went around and saw Clover bent over and wiping her mouth with the sleeve of her sweatshirt.

"Oh God." Clover's eyes were watery. "I just stepped in dog poop. It's, like, fresh. And it stinks."

Ernestine scanned the grass. Dog shit was everywhere. "Here, let me have your shoe. I'll wash it off. You go in, I'll finish up." Clover hobbled to the door of the RV and went inside.

Ernestine completed the hookups and took Clover's shoe to a nearby faucet. Gagging, she was reminded of why she'd never wanted to own a dog. When she was a kid, folks just let their dogs run and do their business wherever, but these days you were expected to keep your dog on a leash and carry poop bags. Apparently the folks camping here didn't do that. As she worked on Clover's shoe, using a stick to get between the treads, Ernestine replayed their conversation about marijuana and wondered where Clover planned to get it.

Setting the shoe aside to dry, Ernestine went inside and found Clover sound asleep on the sofa. Swallowing her disappointment, she fixed a light supper for Walter and resigned herself to the fact that getting marijuana wasn't going to happen. She supposed it was a stupid idea anyway.

"What's wrong with Linda?" Walter asked, seeing Clover asleep at dinnertime. "Is she sick?"

"It's not Linda, Walter, it's Clover."

"Is she sick?"

"No. She's just tired."

"Is she sick? Is Linda sick?"

"No. She's just tired."

He was getting agitated. "What's wrong with Linda?"

Changing tactics, Ernestine said, "she has a headache and I gave her some aspirin." Neither of those things was true, but the lie seemed to work. By nine o'clock he'd stopped asking and had gone to bed.

Exhausted, Ernestine sat alone at the table. She'd been fired-up about getting some marijuana and wondered if there were, in fact, campers right under her nose that had some. She put on a jacket and picked up a flashlight. Then, with Chip on his leash, she crept down the steps, careful not to wake Walter or Clover. Sweeping the light across the grass to make sure she didn't step in anything, she headed down the road.

It was quiet, as though everyone had settled in for the night. She stopped to let Chip pee and heard laughter, so she followed the sound. As she got closer, she smelled wood smoke and another odor she couldn't identify.

Then she saw them, a group of young people sitting around a campfire, passing around a cigarette. They all wore jeans, t-shirts, and those strappy sandals, Chacos, she thought they were called. Ernestine guessed they were all in their early twenties. One kid had a splotchy beard, and a couple of the others had shoulder-length hair. There appeared to be only two girls, but one of the long-haired kids could have been female, she couldn't tell. When she approached, they shifted nervously as if they expected trouble. Then the two girls spotted the puppy and came over to pet him.

"He's so cute," one said. "What's his name?"

"Chip."

"How old is he?"

"About four and a half months." Ernestine stood for a few minutes and let the girls pet the pup. "Are you all traveling together?"

No one answered, so she pointed in the direction of the Allegro. "That's us in that big rig over there. I was just out for a walk and wondered who my neighbors were." She started to turn. "I'd better get back. My husband is sick."

"What's wrong with him?" one of the girls asked.

"I'm not a hundred percent sure, but he's confused and whatever he has makes him really anxious."

Ernestine thought she heard someone say, "Bummer."

She hesitated, took a few steps toward the motorhome, and then doubled back. "Actually, I was wondering if that," she waived her hand in the direction of the passing cigarette, "is marijuana you're smoking. I'd like to know where I could get some for my husband. I've heard it helps with anxiety."

For a minute no one spoke, and Ernestine wondered if she'd made a mistake. Maybe it wasn't marijuana, or it was and they were going to deny it.

"We can give you some." It was one of the girls.

"Really? Oh that would be..."

The brightness of the campfire darkened everything not in its circle, and it wasn't until the girl started to walk back toward the trees that Ernestine noticed the old trailer. When the girl came back, she was carrying a small plastic bag.

"Here," she said handing it to Ernestine. "I put in some rolling papers, too. Do you know how to roll a joint?"

Ernestine took the bag. "Oh thank you. I think we can figure it out. Can I pay you?"

The girl looked around at the others. "Nah, it's okay. I hope it helps him."

When Ernestine got back to the RV, Clover was awake and looking worried. "Where did you go?"

"For a walk." She pulled the bag out of her pocket. "Look what I have."

"Oh my God, Ernie. Where did you get that?"

"I was talking to some nice young people and they gave it to me."

"You shouldn't have done that. You should've waited for me."

"I didn't want to wake you."

"I wasn't going to get it from strangers. I was going to find a store, so you could, like, buy some."

"A store? You can buy it in stores?"

"Yeah, you know all those green crosses we saw? Those are pot stores. Green for marijuana. Cross, like the Red Cross. You know?"

"Oh dear." Ernestine felt herself blush. "I didn't know about that."

"Well anyway," Clover laughed, "Doesn't matter now, does it?"

39

Ernestine's mind wasn't on the morning chores. She remembered to feed the kitten, but forgot to clean the litter box. The milk she'd gotten out for breakfast sat on the counter until lunch time when she realized it wouldn't be any good and threw it away. Even though they hated to lose time, she and Clover had decided to stay an extra night in Glenwood Springs so they could try the marijuana on Walter here, where it was quiet and there weren't many people. Around sundown was when he tended to get anxious, so Ernestine wanted to have dinner over with by then. Worrying about how to approach him with the idea made the day seem endless. She was sure he'd refuse, and hoped Clover could convince him to try.

As soon as they finished dinner, Clover found some soft music on the radio, dimmed the interior lights, and scooted in close beside Walter at the dinette table. Looking uncomfortable, he tried to get up, but she scooted even closer and began stroking his arm. "Tell me about yourself," she said. "What did you like to do when you were my age?"

Walter looked at her and then Ernestine, but he didn't say anything.

Clover went on, "Did you ever smoke marijuana?"

"Oh sure," he said.

Ernestine gasped. "Walter! You never told me that!"

He smiled. "You never asked."

"What do you mean, I never asked? Why would I ask?"

"Why would I tell you?"

Dumbfounded, Ernestine said, "When? When did you?"

"Hunting trips with the guys."

She felt the betrayal like a kick in the gut. She'd never begrudged him the hunting trips he took every fall. In fact she'd been glad he had a chance to get away and relax, even though he couldn't take time for a family vacation. So who was this person? The Walter she knew was totally opposed to marijuana. He was the one who lectured Linda on its dangers. He was the one who grounded her for a month when they discovered pot in her room. What else had he done, she wondered, that he hadn't told her about?

Seething with resentment, she watched Clover open the baggy, empty some of the weed onto one of the papers, pick it up, lick along the edge, roll it and twist the ends.

Walter leaned in as she did it. "Is it good stuff?" Clover passed the joint to him and lit it. He took a long drag, inhaled, held it in and then blew smoke. "Niiiice," he said holding the joint out to Ernestine. She pushed it away and watched him take another hit.

"Okay, dammit," she said after watching him for a while, "give it to me." She took a puff and started coughing. "Wooo," she said, "that burned."

"Take it in slower," Walter said, "and hold it in."

"What are you?" she said, "a pro?" She tried again, slower, and didn't cough. "I don't feel anything."

"You will. Give it time."

Clover watched, looking amused, while Walter and Ernestine passed the joint back and forth.

"I can feel it now, I think," Ernestine giggled. "I feel something ... in my brain. You know, Wal-ter, I'm very hungry at you."

"Me too," he said. "Do we have any tookies?"

"No, I'm hungry... I mean angry. I'm very angry at you."

Walter leaned over and kissed her cheek. "Don't be ... mad."

Ernestine giggled again. "I am very angry ... but right now... I don't remember why." She stood up.

"Where're you going?" he asked. "Come back."

She opened the pantry, got a package of cookies and a bag of potato chips and brought them to the table. Then she started singing along with the radio. "Gonna take a sentimental ...something ... la la laa... I looove that song, don't you, Walter?" She got up and pulled on his hand. "Come on, dance with me."

With the second or third tug on his arm, she managed to get him on his feet, but he teetered and fell backward, pulling her along with him. They collapsed, laughing, on the bench where he shrank against the upholstery with a silly grin on his face and ate more cookies and Ernestine tried to get control of her hysterics. When she did, she couldn't remember what she was laughing at.

40

The evening had been an eye-opener but Ernestine had no desire to try marijuana again. She had, however, gotten over her fear of it. Walter, of course, didn't remember it at all.

Preoccupied with the marijuana idea, Ernestine had driven from Delta to Glenwood Springs with relative ease, but now the road seized her attention again. She drove through Glenwood Canyon, gripping the steering wheel until her knuckles turned white. The rocky cliffs, like enormous layer cakes, boxed her in. The bold reds and purples blurred her vision, and she didn't dare turn her head.

The motorhome coughed and gagged its way toward Loveland Pass and the mile-long Eisenhower Tunnel. Once inside the tunnel, there was nothing to see except white overhead lights in a rounded concrete tube and it seemed to go on forever. Claustrophobic, Ernestine felt tightness in her chest and she began to sweat. As hard as Chip's barking was on her nerves, Walter's keening was worse. She wished they'd given him another joint to smoke this morning.

After clearing the tunnel, the sharp six-percent downhill grade had her pumping the brakes most of the way to Denver. On the outskirts of town, she turned into the first Denny's she came to. Her legs felt so weak that she had to hold onto the door frame for a long time before stepping down.

"Why don't you and Walter go on into the restaurant?" she told Clover, "I'll take Chip. We both need to walk." There was a slight trace of snow on the ground, and hoping the cold, crisp air would clear her head, she put the puppy on his leash and headed for some bushes near the side of the building. After Chip had done his business and she'd disposed of his poop, they continued to walk along the edge of the road. Something in her didn't want to go back.

When at last she joined them in the restaurant, Walter was arguing with the waitress, saying he hadn't ordered the Grand Slam she had placed in front of him.

"It's not what I ordered!" he said slamming his fist on the table. "Not what I ordered." The poor waitress, by all appearances very new to the job, looked like she was about to cry.

Ernestine wanted to scream at him. Instead, she put her head on the table and stayed that way for a very long time. She could hear his tirade, hear Clover trying to help. When she finally sat up, her face was red and creased like it had been pressed between the pages of a heavy book.

"What's wrong," Walter asked. "Is something wrong?"

She didn't answer because she couldn't. Of course something was wrong. She'd just navigated the scariest road ever, and he was causing a ruckus by yelling at a waitress for bringing him food he ordered. Why didn't he know what was wrong? Why didn't he understand anything?

An older waitress approached the table asking if there was a problem and Walter, now eating his Grand Slam, assured her everything was good.

No longer hungry, Ernestine went to the restroom and splashed cold water on her face. "I've never driven in a big city," she said when she returned, "but I'm going to have to do this aren't I?"

The freeway through Denver was almost as terrifying as driving through the mountains. She stayed right, but several times found the lane unexpectedly becoming exit-only. The upside of bumper to bumper traffic was how slowly it moved, the downside was trying to merge the thirty-seven-foot-long vehicle into the left lane.

"Put your blinker on," Clover said. "Sooner or later, someone will let you in."

Ernestine's concentration was such that when Walter yelled, "Where the hell are we?" she jerked the wheel, lost her chance to merge, and found herself on Highway

287 headed toward Mile High Stadium and the stadium parking lot. Cars, buses, and a sea of pedestrian traffic came at her from all directions. She didn't know what to do, where to go, or where she could turn around. "Shit, shit, shit," she groaned.

"Don't panic," Clover said. "Stop and let me out. I'll guide you."

Unsure of what Clover was about to do, Ernestine stopped. Under different circumstances it might have been funny—a pretty blond girl, hugely pregnant, standing in the middle of the Denver Broncos' parking lot, motioning for Ernestine to drive forward, back up, forward again, back up—over and over until she managed to jockey her way out of the tight spot she'd gotten herself into. "Jesus, God," she breathed, "I hope I never have to do that again."

She made her way back to I-70 where the relief of escaping the parking lot was cut short by the onslaught of rush hour traffic.

"What happened?" Walter whined, "Aren't we going to a football game?"

41

The Great Plains east of Denver were a pleasant surprise. Having gotten through the suburb of Aurora, Ernestine once again felt in control. The highway was flat and straight without a single hairpin curve or drop-off anywhere. The broad expanse of land covered with prairie grass reminded her of the Laura Ingalls Wilder's books she'd read as a young girl. Exhaling, she sped up and looked over at Clover. "I think we're almost to Kansas."

It was getting dark, and except for the foray into the Broncos' parking lot, Walter hadn't been awake much at all. Ernestine asked Clover to trade places with him. "Maybe sitting up front with me will keep him awake." She thought perhaps his sleepiness had something to do with the road being so boring, but that didn't explain his lethargy even when they'd been in the mountains.

Deep in thought, she hadn't seen the pothole, and her left front wheel hit it causing the motorhome to sway. Instead of steadying himself, Walter tipped so far to the left that he would have fallen completely off the seat if it hadn't been for the seatbelt. When Ernestine put her arm out and pushed him back, he toppled to the right, landing against the door. She grabbed his arm. "Walter, sit up!" It was like trying to straighten a ragdoll.

"Huh?"

"Sit up."

"Huh?"

"Are you awake?"

"I'm awake. What's the matter?"

"You scared me. It was like you were unconscious or something." She kept glancing over every couple of minutes to see if he was staying upright. It was maybe ten minutes before he spoke again.

"Where are we?"

"We're almost to Kansas."

"Why are we going to Kansas?"

"We're taking Clover to Kansas."

"Does Linda live in Kansas?"

"No, Clover's mother does. We're taking her there."

"Why are we going to Kansas?"

"We're taking Clover to her mother. In Kansas."

"Does Linda live in Kansas?"

"No, Walter. Linda doesn't live in Kansas. Clover does." It was exhausting.

"Are we going home?"

At least it was a different question. "Not yet," she said. "We're not going home yet."

"When are we going home? I want to go home."

"Soon. First we'll take Clover to Kansas. Then we'll go home."

"I want to go home."

Clover reached from behind and massaged Walter's shoulders. "Walter," her voice was soft, "you'll go home soon. Real soon."

He turned and smiled. "Okay, good," he said. "That'll be good."

42

"Oh my God," Ernestine said. "I just realized we're going to be crossing the state line and we have marijuana with us. Isn't that illegal?"

"Yeah. I think it's, like, a felony. You can go to jail for, like, less than an ounce."

"What should we do? We can't get rid of it. We need it for Walter."

"Look, it's okay. Nobody's going to suspect you."

"Why not? Why wouldn't they? You said lots of old people use it."

Clover stood up, put her hands on the small of her back, and stretched. "I just don't think they would. But if you're, like, worried, we can hide it."

"Where?"

"Well, this dude I know told me you can hide it in coffee."

"What do you mean?"

"You could, like, bury it in coffee grounds."

Ernestine looked at Clover in the rearview mirror.

"Okay. There's a full can of coffee in the pantry."

Clover took what was left of the weed, wound it up in several layers of plastic wrap, and shoved it deep into the can.

"Do you think it'll work?" Ernestine asked.

"Hope so," Clover chuckled. "Otherwise, we'll all go to jail."

"I don't think that's funny," Ernestine said.

"Sorry."

Three hours later a nervous but determined Ernestine crossed the border with approximately two grams of contraband hidden in her Folgers can.

At Kanarado, an almost treeless town claiming a population of 153 people, they were hit by a windstorm. Gusts slammed into the side of the Allegro, making it hard for Ernestine to hold it steady, and the wind kicked up so much dust that the road, at times, seemed to disappear.

"Is this common in Kansas?"

"Duh," Clover said. "This is Wizard of Oz country. Like, you know that movie, right?"

Every couple of minutes, a new blast hit and pushed the RV sideways and Ernestine's arms started to ache from the effort of staying on the pavement. Chip, apparently sensing the electrical current from the lightning, curled up under Walter's feet and whimpered.

"This isn't a tornado, is it?"

"No," Clover said. "It's just a wind storm."

The gusts kept coming, and Ernestine, not reassured by Clover's calm, gripped harder on the steering wheel. "We need to get out of this wind."

"There's a place close by where my dad took us camping once. I think I remember how to get there."

The driveway into the park in Colby was strewn with tree limbs and branches, and the wind was blowing with such force that the few insubstantial trees whipped around like a cowhand's lasso. Ernestine barely made it to the office and back without being knocked down.

The set-up was difficult with the wind pushing them around. When they finished, Clover gathered a clean set of clothes and some toiletries.

Ernestine watched her, long blond hair flying, back arched and belly forward, lurch across the lawn to the bathhouse. She turned to Walter, "I have a feeling she's going into labor tonight."

43

"Ernestine. Ernestine!"

Ernestine sat up and grabbed her bathrobe. It was 3:00 a.m. She came out of the bedroom to find Clover on her hands and knees on the sofa, rocking back and forth.

"It hurts. Oh, it hurts."

"Okay, honey," Ernestine put her hand on Clover's back. "Breathe like I showed you. Are the pains close together?"

"Uh-huh."

Ernestine got Walter's wristwatch from the bedroom. "We're going to time them now. You tell me when the next one comes." She grabbed the phone, called 911, and gave the name of the campground and her space number. "We have a girl here in labor. We don't have a car." Then she got dressed and woke Walter. "Put on some clothes, we're having a baby." By the time the ambulance arrived, Clover's contractions were three minutes apart and lasting from sixty to ninety seconds.

Four a.m. was a quiet time in the Citizen's Medical Center waiting room. In a strange place and unaccustomed to being up at this hour, Walter circled the room, sat down, got up and circled the room some more. "What are we doing here?" he asked over and over, even though Ernestine's answer was the same every time. When he said he was hungry, she gave him some dollar bills and pointed him toward a bank of vending machines. In the three hours before the cafeteria opened, Walter ate three packages of cookies, two bags of M&M's, and two Kit Kat bars. At seven, the loudspeaker crackled, "The cafeteria is open," and Ernestine led him to the elevator.

"No," he said, "I want to go back."

"Back where?"

"That room where we were before."

There was another couple in the waiting room now, probably waiting for a grandchild. They eyed Walter warily as he continued to fidget and pace. Ernestine smiled at them hoping they would understand, but by the time the young doctor in scrubs pushed through the double doors, she was ready to choke him.

"Mother and baby are doing fine," the doctor said. It's a boy. Seven pounds, fourteen ounces."

Walter shook the doctor's hand, but the look on his face was utter confusion. Ernestine wondered if he understood what had just happened.

44

Clover lowered the baby into the improvised bassinet Ernestine made by taking a drawer from a cabinet in the RV and padding it with receiving blankets. Walter stood nearby, watching the baby grunt and squirm and wave his tiny fists. He touched the baby's downy head.

"What's his name?"

"Walter," Clover said, smiling at the old man. "Walter William Andrews. I named him after you."

Walter looked stunned. "Did you say Walter, after me?"

"Yes, Walter for you, and William for my grandpa."

The old man's eyes glistened and his voice cracked. "Can I hold him?" He sat in the rocker and Clover laid the baby in his arms. It was all Ernestine could do to hold back her own tears. She knew Clover had grown fond of Walter, but she'd never expected her to name the baby after him.

The sight of Walter with the newborn baby in his arms brought back the memory of the day Linda was born. Walter had been on a hunting trip when she went into labor, and she'd had no way to reach him. She got word to her older brother, who drove nearly fifty miles to find Walter and bring him to the hospital. By the time he arrived, so had Linda. Ernestine could still see him in his camouflage shirt, dirty jeans, and bright orange cap, holding his tiny daughter and crying. It was the sweetest, most tender moment of her life. And here Walter was, eighty years old, holding a baby boy that had been given his name. She hoped the moment would last for him, that he would remember it tomorrow.

They didn't leave the campground right away. Clover spent most of the next three days holding her baby, watching him sleep, learning to tell when he was hungry, when his tummy hurt, and when he was filling his diaper. She laughed at his funny little noises, sang to him, and told him she was going to be the best mommy in the world.

When coaching was necessary, Ernestine stepped in to show Clover how to hold the baby for nursing, how to care for her nipples to keep them from cracking and getting sore, and how to keep the baby's umbilical cord stump clean and dry. But while she did these things, her heart ached knowing she was about to lose them both.

Displaced, Chip whimpered and begged for attention. Clover talked to him and petted him, but it was clear things had changed. He was no longer allowed to jump up on Clover's lap and he got scolded when he got too close to the baby. Even Walter wasn't paying him as much attention as before the baby came. The kitten, larger now, jumped up to look at the baby but kept getting shooed away.

By the fourth day, Ernestine accepted it was time to move on to Manhattan. Outside, the sun was shining. There was no wind and she took her time disconnecting the hoses and cords. She knew they had to leave, but her heart wasn't in it. Clover was more than a lost teenager who needed help. She'd become a friend, a confidant—almost a daughter. Ernestine didn't know how she would get by without her, but she would have to. Clover needed to get on with her own life—be with her own mother.

45

The day had started out clear and sunny but behind her as she drove Ernestine could see storm clouds gathering. By mid-morning the sky was the color of pewter. In the rear-view mirror, she made eye-contact with Clover.

"How close are we?"

"It's, like, maybe another hour."

Ernestine glanced at Walter in the seat beside her. He hadn't spoken in over an hour but his eyes were open and he was looking around. "I think we're going to get caught in a storm," she said. "Do you see how black those clouds are?"

The words were barely out of her mouth when huge raindrops began hammering the motorhome. She turned the windshield wipers on high speed where they slapped furiously but made no difference. It was impossible to see the road. In front of her, cars with their flashers on were pulling off to the side. She searched the instrument panel for her flashers, pushed the button, and pulled in behind the line of cars.

"What's going on?" Walter asked. "Why are we stopping?"

"Look how hard it's raining. I can't see to drive."

Then the rain stopped as suddenly as it had started, and it began to hail. Huge stones hit and bounced, turning everything snowy white.

"My Lord," Ernestine said when the hail stopped, "I've never seen anything like this."

"You've never lived in Kansas," Clover said.

Ernestine took a deep breath, put the motorhome in gear and, fish-tailing on the slick pavement, pulled back onto the highway. The road stayed wet but the sun came out and gradually the landscape began to change. Soon they were seeing foothills blanketed with tall, bronze-colored grass.

Behind her, Clover was nursing the baby. Ernestine could hear his whimpers, the smacking of his lips. It amused her how eager he was, how hungry. He was only a few days old and filling out already.

"This is beautiful country," she said looking around. "I thought Kansas was all flat."

"That's what everybody thinks. It's not, though."

"What is that out there?"

"It's called a tallgrass prairie."

"It's beautiful. Do you suppose there's a place to stop? I really should get Walter out to walk a bit."

"There's the Konza Prairie Biological Center. It's real close."

"What is that?"

"A research center. We went there on a field trip when I was in middle school. It's, like, really cool."

"Perfect. Is it okay with you if we stop for a few minutes?"

"Sure," Clover said. "It's your call."

Ernestine parked the motorhome and handed Walter his cane. "Come on, dear, let's take a walk."

"Where are we?" he asked. "What is this place?"

"It's a research center. Can you see the grass out there?"

"Grass?"

"Yes. Prairie grass. Let's get out and look."

Ever since Walter's fall, it had gotten harder and harder to get him in and out of the motorhome. The long step down was especially challenging. Ernestine had to get out first and let him lean against her for balance. It was scary knowing he might fall and that she might not be able to catch him. But scary or not, he needed to walk. The doctor had warned, "It only takes a few days of inactivity to lose muscle strength, and a lot longer to get it back," She worried about how weak he'd gotten, worried about all the time spent in the motorhome. All he did was sit. Or sleep. Mostly sleep.

Easing him down the steps, she thought again about how quickly their roles had changed. He'd always been the protector, the knight in shining armor who threw his coat over puddles. Now she was doing that for him.

Clover, carrying little Wally, climbed out after them and called the puppy. "Come Chip, come." He jumped down, excitedly wagging his tail. Holding Wally in one arm, she bent down and slipped the leash over Chip's head.

With Walter at her side, Ernestine read the different informational markers. One informed her that this was an 8,616-acre tallgrass prairie preserve operated by Kansas State University. Another marker had a map of the Nature Trail Loop which it showed winding for two and a half miles through forests, crossing a creek, and climbing over limestone ledges. "We're not doing that," she said, opting for an easier path where the grass on both sides was taller than their heads. Gazing at the massive expanse of rippling grasses, she thought how diverse the country was, and how little she'd seen of it. It hadn't been her idea to buy the motorhome, or take this trip, but if they hadn't, she would never have seen this part of the country. And she wouldn't have met Clover.

Wishing they could stay longer, Ernestine gave in to Walter's limping and turned around. As they got closer to where she'd parked the motorhome, she saw Clover sitting on a bench near the main building. Backlit by the afternoon sun, she was wrapped in a halo of light, and Ernestine was reminded that in a few short miles, a few short minutes, she would be losing this girl who had come to mean so much to her.

Certain that Clover had seen her and Walter return to the motorhome, Ernestine waited for her to join them.

When she didn't, Ernestine left Walter and walked to where Clover sat staring into space.

"Are you scared?"

"Yeah, I guess. I haven't seen my mom in, like, forever."

Ernestine slid onto the bench. "You know, you haven't told me a whole lot about your mom other than she left and you lived with your dad. Is there something more I should know?"

"I don't know much about her, either. She, like, never came to visit us or anything."

"What does she do? Does she work?"

"I dunno."

"Does your dad keep in touch with her?"

"I...I think so. Maybe. He's the one who gave me her address." She pulled a wrinkled piece of paper out of her pocket and wadded it up in her fist.

"Are you sure this is what you want?" Ernestine asked.

Clover kissed the baby's head and heaved herself up from the bench. "Yes. Let's go. I can find directions on the phone."

46

Entering the town of Manhattan, Ernestine's eyes scanned the streets. The mature trees, stately homes, and university campus weren't at all what she'd expected out here in the middle of the country. She wouldn't have been able to say why, but somehow, it gave her an entirely different notion of what kind of person Clover's mother might be, and she began to question her own biases. There could be all kinds of reasons a woman might leave her children. If the father was in a better position to raise them, or if her career demanded she be in a bigger city. Never having had a calling of her own, she wondered if she'd be less critical of the woman if she had. Still, she couldn't excuse the woman for not seeing her daughters for six years.

The town, however, seemed to offer opportunity. Maybe with her mom's help, Clover could go back to school. Finish her education. She was a smart girl and she could be successful if given the chance.

"Do you think we're close?" she asked.

Clover looked up from the phone where she was mapping the route. "It's quite a ways yet."

As they left the nicer part of town, Ernestine's hopes began to dwindle. It was still good, she thought, that Clover would be reunited with her mother, but less likely that her economic status would improve.

The address was in a neighborhood with no sidewalks, where cars were parked alongside ditches, and yards were mostly weeds. Slowing to read house numbers, Ernestine pulled up to the curb. "This must be it."

The house was a single story, set far back on the lot. An older model Cadillac was parked in the carport. A bicycle with a flat tire was leaning against it, giving the impression that neither had been moved in a while.

Clover sat motionless for a few minutes and then slowly began moving her belongings closer to the door of the RV. When Ernestine and Walter had first picked her up, she'd only had a backpack and a puppy. Now her possessions had grown to include a baby, a car seat, and two big bags of baby stuff.

Finished gathering, she stepped between the front seats and put her arms around Walter. "I'm really gonna miss you."

Walter smiled and patted her shoulder. "You too," he said. "You too."

Holding back tears, Ernestine got up from the driver's seat, lifted Wally and cradled him in her arms. Holding him this way, parallel to the ground, she felt his back curve, and his little body relax. She studied his face, memorizing the tiny features, smelling his smell, and dreaded the moment she'd have to let him go.

Clover stepped out of the RV and set all her things on the grass. Ernestine kissed the baby and passed him to Clover. "You go on now," she said. "See your mom. I'll keep an eye on your things."

"I don't know how I can ever thank you. You and Walter have been so nice."

"You don't need to thank us," Ernestine said, giving her a hug. "We've loved having you."

Clover started toward the house, stopping halfway to look back. At the door, she straightened her shoulders and rang the bell. When no one answered right away, she shifted the baby in her arms, looked at Ernestine, and rang the bell again.

Ernestine picked up the pup, petted him, and continued to watch. Minutes went by before the door opened.

"Well, I'll be god-damned." The voice was loud and harsh.

"Hi, Mom."

Flicking the ash from her cigarette, the woman scowled at the bundle in Clover's arms. "So, you got yourself knocked up, did you?"

Clover flinched. "I-I thought you'd want to meet your grandson."

271

"Why would I want to do that?"

Clover backed up a step. "Because he's..."

"He's what?"

"He's your ... your grandson, Mom."

"What do you want?"

Clover pulled the baby closer, and her voice shook. "I hoped we... just until..."

"Until what? Until you find some other sucker to take care of you?" The woman raised her chin in the direction of Ernestine. "Who's that?"

"Ernestine. Her and her husband brought me here. They've been so nice..."

"Well, they can keep on being nice, because you're not bringing your trouble into this house."

"Mom?"

"If I wanted to raise babies, I would have stayed with your father." The door slammed, and Clover was left on the step clutching her baby.

The woman's cruel, ugly words, made Ernestine feel sick. How could a mother—even remembering the hurtful things she'd said to her own daughter—how could a mother turn her daughter away?

Ernestine watched Clover stand there, not reaching to ring the bell again, not turning toward the motorhome, and knew with absolute clarity what to do.

She put the pup and Clover's belongings back inside the motorhome and went to where Clover was standing, "Come on, honey," she said. "Let's go home."

Two and a half years later...

Ernestine put her pocketbook on the kitchen counter next to several large bouquets and dropped onto a chair. "Whew, I'm exhausted."

"It was a lovely service, Mom." Linda stood near the sink, looking at the picture on the front of a program. "It was nice to see so many of Dad's friends there."

"It was, wasn't it? And so many of his customers from the store. They had such glowing things to say about him."

It was warm in the kitchen and the heavy scent of lilies was overpowering. "Jack and Jeremy," Ernestine said, "would you do your grandma a favor and take these flowers out to the living room? The fragrance is giving me a headache."

With the flowers out of the way, Ernestine started removing covered dishes from a picnic hamper and putting them in the refrigerator. "Just look at all this food," she said to Linda. "When you and Matt leave, I want you to take most of it with you. It'll just go to waste here."

After everything was put away, Ernestine asked Linda and Matt to sit down. "There's something I want you to have." She left the room and when she returned, she handed Linda an envelope and a set of keys.

"They're for the motorhome," she said. "That thing has been sitting in the driveway since we got home from the trip, and I have no desire drive it again. I've transferred the title to you."

"But..."

"No. No buts. You kids take it and enjoy it. It's what Walter would want."

Linda stood, teary eyed, and gave Ernestine a long, tight hug. "I don't know what to say."

"Just enjoy. Take a family vacation. Jack will be going off to college soon and this might be your last chance to do something together. I just wish your dad and I had done that with you."

Linda nodded and wiped her eyes. "So what are your plans now that Dad's gone?"

Ernestine smiled. "Well, I'm going to get a job."

"A job? Didn't Dad leave you enough—?"

"Oh, it's not that. I'm in pretty good shape in that regard. Do you remember your dad's financial advisor, Clyde Bullock?"

Linda looked skeptical. "Of course."

"He's offered me a job in his office, as soon as I'm ready."

"But, Mom, are you sure that's a good idea? Shouldn't you give yourself time to grieve?"

Ernestine took Linda's hand, "Honey, you need to understand, I lost your dad a long time ago. I've done my grieving."

"Oh, Mom, I'm so sorry."

"I'm sorry too. But I'm still here and I want to do something interesting with the time I have left."

"But finance?"

"Why is that so surprising? I've been managing our portfolio ... well, ever since your dad couldn't."

"But, you'll need to use computers and you can't—"

"Can't what? Use a computer? I've been taking classes."

"You have? While you were caring for Dad? How'd you—?"

"Clover was here. She took care of Walter when I was gone, and I took care of Wally when she was."

Linda shook her head. "You're full of surprises."

Just then Wally ran through the kitchen, chasing the dog. Ernestine caught the boy and pulled him close. His jacket was twisted and his shirt tail was out.

"Look at you," she said finger-combing his blond hair. "I wanted your mommy to see how handsome you looked in your suit. Now you're all messy."

"No." Wally dislodged himself from her grasp and followed Chip to his food dish in the corner of the kitchen. At the sound of Clover's car in the driveway, Chip left his bowl and ran to greet her. When the petting and licking and tail wagging stopped, Clover went to where Linda and Matt were sitting and gave them each a hug. "I'm so sorry I missed the service. I really wanted to be there, but new hires at the hospital don't get to choose their shifts."

"Wally was there in your place, dear," Ernestine said. "He looked so handsome in his little suit."

"And he charmed everyone," Linda added. "Especially when he announced 'Nobody should cry, cause Papa just went to see Jesus.'"

Clover picked up Wally to give him a kiss, but he wiggled free.

"You have a surprise, too, don't you, dear," Ernestine prompted.

Shyly, Clover held out her left hand. Everyone, including Jack and Jeremy, crowded in to get a look at the ring and offer congratulations.

"Life," Matt said, not remembering who he was quoting, "the next thing, then the next, then the next."

The End

About the Author

Ellen Gardner has lived in various parts of the western US her entire life. She now resides in Ashland, Oregon with her husband, Jerry Hauck, whom she met in a support group when both their former spouses were suffering from Alzheimer's disease. Now free to travel, they do their best to make up for lost time. When they aren't traveling, they are "paying forward" by facilitating support groups for other caregivers.

Ellen's first book, *Veda, a novel,* is available at Amazon.com in paperback and Kindle versions.

Made in the USA
Lexington, KY
15 September 2018